THE MAN FROM NOWHERE

Center Point
Large Print

**This Large Print Book carries the
Seal of Approval of N.A.V.H.**

THE MAN FROM NOWHERE

T. V. Olsen

CENTER POINT LARGE PRINT
THORNDIKE, MAINE

This Center Point Large Print edition
is published in the year 2019 by arrangement with
Golden West Literary Agency.

Originally published in the US by Ace Books.
Originally published in the UK by Thorpe.

The text of this Large Print edition is unabridged.
In other aspects, this book may vary
from the original edition.
Printed in the United States of America
on permanent paper.
Set in 16-point Times New Roman type.

ISBN: 978-1-64358-169-9 (hardcover)
ISBN: 978-1-64358-173-6 (softcover)

Library of Congress Cataloging-in-Publication Data

Names: Olsen, Theodore V., author.
Title: The man from nowhere / T.V. Olsen.
Description: Center Point Large Print edition. | Thorndike, Maine :
    Center Point Large Print, 2019.
Identifiers: LCCN 2019001652| ISBN 9781643581699 (hardcover :
    alk. paper) | ISBN 9781643581736 (paperback : alk. paper)
Subjects: LCSH: Large type books. | GSAFD: Western stories.
Classification: LCC PS3565.L8 M295 2019 | DDC 813/.54—dc23
LC record available at https://lccn.loc.gov/2019001652

CHAPTER ONE

At first there were five of them. Five who rode up from the south, into the foothills of the Wyoming Absarokas. Five stony-faced, weather-stained men who rode slack and easy in the saddle like all men bred to horseback, but whose eyes were narrow-tense and hard and skin-crinkled at the outer corners from a long habit of watchfulness. All were alike in these ways, although in age they ranged from white-haired Bowie Samse's fifty-eight to the twenty-odd years of "the kid," Johnny Vano.

They'd ridden for a long time through drought-parched country, but it was a day for ducks when they hit the foothills. All morning swift clouds with dark swollen underbellies scudded the drab sky. Shortly after the noon stop the rain began, catching the five riders in the open. Four of them wanted to find shelter, but their leader, Sam Vano, inexorable, absolute, and always sure, kept them heading north into pale, slashing torrents of water that whipped in windlashed gusts against the leaning forms of horses and men. No brief blow, and they rode it out. A day-long siege of it.

Even in high-buttoned slickers, they were soaked, miserable, and ugly-tempered when, toward evening, a densely-timbered rise of ground loomed ahead and Sam Vano called a halt. They put their horses directly toward the heart of the scrub oak stand, and broke into a wide clearing. Sam looked around and dismounted with a grunt of satisfaction. They'd be well-hidden here, which was all that concerned him. The mutinous, surly grumblings of the others couldn't make Sam bat an eyelash; he knew his men, knew that they'd be lost without him, and that they knew it too.

They made a cold, wet camp—a misery camp. The rain had begun to slacken away into a gray drizzle. Young Johnny Vano threw saddle, saddlebags, and canvas-wrapped blanket roll from his sorrel, and lugged them over to the leeward side of a looming granite outcrop. Where the rock had checked the blast of wind and rain it was reasonably dry. With a saddle-weary grunt, Johnny dropped his gear and sat down on his bedroll, stretching his thin arms. He didn't rest long, for shortly Sam Vano was yelling for him to build a fire.

What with, and how? Johnny wondered sourly, but knew better than to question his father's orders aloud. A full-armed slap of a hard-calloused palm was Sam Vano's wordless reply to filial rebellion. Resignedly Johnny got stiffly to his feet and made a circle of the clearing, limbering his legs and arms.

When he chanced to glance over at his rock, he saw that his cousin, Jesse Norcross, was kicking Johnny's gear out into the rain, appropriating the lee side for himself. Johnny's hands balled into fists and he started across the clearing, choking, "Damn you, Jess!"

Jesse's long-limbered, cat-lithe body swung to face him, with the bubbling laugh that showed chalk-white teeth and never reached his eyes. He whipped off his hat, batting the wet felt against the shining wetness of his brush-chaps and tossing it on his other gear. The rain matted Jesse's crisp black hair, roached like a mule's mane, and he ran a hand over it in a slicking-back motion, handsome face still laughing.

"You don't like it, tiger, you know what to do."

Jesse was several years Johnny's senior. Fast with his fists and guns, faster with the women, he knew just how to needle the kid and always tried.

Choked with rage, Johnny dived headlong for the slim, mocking figure, and Jesse made a fluid sideward step and Johnny burgeoned past and plowed on his face in the littered gear. Instantly he lunged to his feet, whirled, went after Jesse again, and Jesse danced away, taunting him. "That's it, tiger, let's see your teeth."

The other men watched disinterestedly. Johnny bored furiously in, swinging wild blows which didn't connect. His boot skidded on the wet loam and his feet, aided by the awkward

7

reactions of his long, gangling body, flailed the ground away and piled him on his face again. He lay there, sobbing in torn breaths. Jesse prodded him tentatively in the side with a boot, laughing. "Come on, tiger, you can do it. No?"

Johnny didn't rise, even after Jesse walked away, whistling, to the rock shelter. He knew that a fight with his cousin would end like all their others; he'd be pummeled to a pulp and Jesse would take what he wanted anyhow.

Finally he pushed himself up on his hands and knees and then to his feet, avoiding the looks of the others. Wet socks squishing in his boots, he walked from the clearing, pushed into a dripping oak thicket and hunkered down there to be alone with his present shame and the memories of a thousand others. He rested his arms on his knees and set his teeth into his slicker sleeve, tasting its oiliness, and listened to the rain pock the leaves above his head.

From the clearing he heard the mildly chiding voice of Bowie Samse. "You hadn't ought to let Jesse maul the kid that way, Sam."

"Growing-up medicine," was Sam Vano's terse reply. "Kid's got to learn to take knocks like the rest of us. No business for cream puffs, this." He lifted his voice. "Johnny! You fetch wood, build up that fire now, hear me?"

Johnny got to his feet and plunged through the brush, heedless of the wet lash of back-whipping branches, till he found a rotten deadfall. With furious energy, he kicked out great chunks of its tinder-dry heart. As he bent to scoop them up, bootsteps thunked solidly across the sodden ground. He looked up at Bowie Samse.

Bowie's slicker hung in loose folds on his shriveled body; there were feverish spots of color in his wasted cheeks, and one clawlike hand smothered a racking cough. Bowie was consumptive. He looked twenty years older than he was, a shadowy ghost of the big, vital man Johnny remembered.

Swift concern touched Johnny. "You're in a bad way."

Bowie gave a dry chuckle. "I'll live." His hollow tone doubted it. He squatted with a grim face, reaching trembling fingers. "Here, I'll help you."

Johnny dug his chin into his collar, said gruffly, "Never mind." He piled up an armload of the rotten heartwood. Bowie rested on his heels. He reached out and tapped bony knuckles against the hard shell of the log. Another dry chuckle. "Sort of like Jess, ain't it? Sound on the outside, bad at the core."

Johnny grunted uneasily. *Watch it,* he told himself; *he's making more fool talk.* Sam Vano would say in one of his rare streaks of almost humorless humor, "Damn Bowie plumb missed his calling. Should've been a sky-pilot." Then

Sam would add, more meaningfully, as a plain warning, "Maybe you're gettin' too old for the game, Bowie?" Sam and Bowie had ridden together for twenty years and more; that gave Bowie some room for liberties that hardbitten Sam Vano wouldn't tolerate from the younger men—but beyond a point, even Bowie didn't step. That line marked Sam's iron-fisted domination of his men; it made dangerous tampering.

Bowie was moodily twirling a twig between his fingers, frowning at it. "I said it before, kid," he told Johnny. "Get out of this rat race before it's too late. You're cut from a different cloth."

"Like you ain't?" Johnny jeered softly. "Like Jesse, Lopez, and Sam ain't? Hell, Bowie, I'm Sam's son. I ain't ashamed of it."

Bowie glanced at him swiftly, scowling, and opened his mouth, then shook his hawkish head as though he'd decided against saying something. But he did grunt, "Difference is, the rest of us, Sam included, all decided long time ago what we'd make of our lives. We had a choice. Being born to it, you never did. Think back once, son. What do you remember . . . ?"

Johnny's busy hands held motionless. He rocked back on his heels, studying on it. A thousand camps like this one, some colder and wetter. Some dry and hungry. Days and often nights of far-ranging, grueling rides in rain, snow, blazing heat, till you'd never known anything but the rocking and jolting back and forth in a sweaty saddle. Weeks stretching into months of holing up in a desert rendezvous or a mountain hideaway, where boredom hung like a dead weight. Riding alone into a hundred towns from Rio to the Canadian border to fetch supplies for the gang, with the feeling that a thousand unseen eyes were boring at your back, expecting any time to feel the heavy hand of a lawman clamp your shoulder. Ten thousand days and nights in company with taciturn, haggard-eyed men who jumped at a sound, hands dropping to well-worn pistol grips. Men who came and went, whom you never got to know and didn't want to.

That was Johnny Vano's life.

"Make good studyin', son?" Bowie broke his thoughts softly.

"Damn it, Bowie," Johnny burst out, "you hush that talk! You know Sam don't—"

"I know Sam a sight better'n you, youngster," Bowie Samse cut him off with a harsh abruptness. "Come on, let's be toting this stuff into camp."

In silence, they trudged to the clearing with armfuls of the crumbling punk, dumping it on a dry place under the widespreading boughs of a gnarled oak. Johnny's mind was an angry turmoil. He wondered if Bowie knew how deeply he'd scored. His words had forced Johnny to face the nameless yearnings that had begun to gnaw in him more and more frequently. Things

11

he had to cover with rough words or surly silence so the others wouldn't see. The trouble was, having known no other life than this, he wasn't sure what his hidden urges amounted to, or how much they meant.

Biting his lip in frustration, he ground a handful of the heartwood between his palms to make a small heap of loose tinder. Over this he built a wigwam of dry twigs he'd gathered from under the log. He reached inside his slicker for the oilcloth-wrapped packet of matches, fumbled one out, struck it alight on a dry patch of his pants, and cupped the orange flare in his palms. Smoke threaded from the tinder, then a spoon of flame which caught the twigs. When he had a steady blaze, Johnny piled on chunks of the rotten wood.

Jesse came across the clearing at a swinging stride, whistling cheerfully, carrying the battered coffee pot full of canteen water. Before Johnny had time to wonder why Jesse was doing a menial chore with a cheerful air, Jesse reached the fire and bent as though to set the pot close by. It tilted in his hand; a stream of water gouted over the meager blaze. The fire sizzled and died in a thin mushrooming of steam and smoke. Johnny came to his feet, no uncertainty in him.

"You did that a-purpose."

Jesse's black brows lifted in the blandest shrug of innocence. "Why tiger, I was trying to help."

Sam Vano strode heavy-footed across the clearing, an emphatic anger in his swinging arms. "Jesse, you're goin' too far, damn it!"

The sodden smack of his fist froze each man in position, except Jesse, who somersaulted backward. He rolled over once and landed on his back. He shook his head. Handsome face distorted, he ripped open his slicker, clawing for his holstered gun.

CHAPTER TWO

Both Vanos, Sam and Johnny, were covering Jesse Norcross with leveled sidearms before he had his clear of its holster. He lay on his back, crafty-bleached eyes gauging his chances and rejecting them, behind those eyes a silent fury still walled, biding its time now.

Sam Vano slammed his gun into its sheath with a contemptuous grunt. Standing well over a bull-shouldered six feet, Sam Vano's face was bone-gaunt, craggy as a mountain, the mouth a thin slash of brown granite. Just the look of him had made more than one hardcase think twice.

"You know better than to brace a man on your back, Jess. Since you're feeling so raunchy, git some more wood and make up that fire. You can cook supper too."

Jesse maneuvered cautiously to one knee, then straight-ended up, baleful eyes following Sam Vano's broad back as he stalked away. Jesse wiped a thin trickle of blood from the corner of his mouth. He stared briefly at Johnny, but didn't say anything. He picked up his hat and walked from the clearing.

Johnny was conscious that he still held the gun. The grips slippery against his palm. He sheathed it slowly. He was realizing that though he and Sam had gotten their slickers open at the same time, that they'd made the draw within a fraction of the instant, his gun had been pointed and cocked while Sam's was still swinging to level. For a moment he felt a wild exultation; long hours of unstinting practice had paid off. He had at last beat Sam, who had a broad reputation with a hand-gun.

Then he noticed that Bowie Samse and Chino Lopez, silent observers, were both watching him steadily from a few yards distance. Lopez had just come from tending the horses, his special detail. He was a Mexican-Ute half-breed, a wolf-gaunt, loosely built man in his middle thirties, whose turgid, ink-black eyes surveyed Johnny stolidly. But Johnny saw Bowie shake his head, very slightly, before he turned away.

Johnny hunkered down against the oak trunk, his back to the wet bark. Bowie's look had the effect of changing his moment of triumph into a gray sense of failure. It was a feeling for which he wouldn't account. Who had he failed, he wondered. Not Bowie, for Bowie was a dying man, full of regret, but past caring about success or failure for his own dwindling days. Himself, then? In a groping, elemental fashion, Johnny reasoned that Bowie saw that ready gun-draw as only another factor that would stand against Johnny if ever he tried to escape this life.

But he thought: *Bowie's a talky old fool. Even if you wanted, there's no turning back.* Sam had said so many a time. His name was known to half the sheriffs and territorial marshals in the West, together with the rest of the Vano gang. *What the hell are you thinking of, letting old Bowie get under your skin with this sky-pilot stuff? Get rid of it!*

It was much the way Sam Vano himself might have rebutted Johnny's thoughts, had he known them. Johnny had never quite understood his own feeling about Sam. Oddly, he rarely thought of the elder Vano as his father. He did admire Sam's rough-and-ready way of tackling a situation, his iron dominance of the men who rode with him; he used Sam's rough judgments of life as his own criteria. He made a hard, even brutal, parent; but Johnny, knowing no other, and with no memory of a mother whom Sam had never mentioned, saw nothing amiss in that. He and his father were not close, yet he'd never questioned the fact of his unswerving loyalty to the man.

Jesse tramped into camp, bearing an armload of dry wood. Without a word he set to building a fire. His hands were shaking with the residue of his fear and fury. Johnny wondered uneasily how wise it had been of Sam to strike Jesse, even to maintain authority.

Jesse, the bastard son of Sam Vano's only

sister and a gambler named Ned Norcross, had been with the gang for eight years. With his own peculiar sense of familial obligation, Sam had taken on the orphaned boy when his mother, Norcross's shill, had died from a stray bullet in a gambling table shoot-out in Abilene. A more purposely aimed slug had taken Ned Norcross's spotty life. As the youngest men of the gang, Johnny and Jesse had been thrown together in a sort of spit-and-claw companionship; there'd been only bad blood between them from the start.

Johnny had long known two things about Jesse: he was a natural bully, and he never forgot a slight. Long since, Sam Vano had earned the ebullient Jesse's resentment with his utter lack of sympathy; tonight Johnny had watched that brimming resentment turn abruptly into deep hatred. Sam had struck him hard, but the lightest of cuffs would have produced the same reaction from Jesse. So Johnny was watchful and uneasy.

The meal was a good one, for Jesse, though hating work, took a perverse pride in doing any job well. He had a magic touch for the crudest of camp fare; even under tonight's miserable conditions, the usual coffee, beans, bacon, and biscuits had never tasted better.

Squatting on their heels around the fire, the men wolfed their food in silence. The drizzle had died away. Numb and chill from hours of cold, beating rain, the men held their hands to

17

the fire and began to dry out. Their mood warmed with their bodies. Bowie told a joke in his dry way, and all, even Jesse, grinned.

Sam Vano stripped off his slicker and rubbed his ham-like hands together. His chipped-rock features had a fitful, ghoulish quality in the flickering light. "Let's get to business."

"Good," growled Bowie Samse. "We ride clear up from Sonora on your say-so that there's a big job waiting "in Wyoming, but you don't breathe a word of what it's to be."

A muscle twitched momentarily at the corner of Vano's vise-like mouth—the closest he ever came to a smile. He clapped Bowie's thin shoulder lightly. Sam's spirits always mounted before he brought a job off, Johnny knew.

Almost a year ago the gang had hit a Texas rancher's herd along the Rio, then had fled south of the border where there was no fear of pursuit, driving several hundred head of the Texan's cattle ahead of them. They'd sold the herd to a *haciendado* in Sonora who asked no questions, then settled down in Hermosillo for a long wait, while the hue and cry back in Texas died down. It was a familiar routine for Sam Vano, one he'd always followed. Hit, and vanish where they can't reach you. Across the Mexican border, or the Canadian, sometimes into the wild back-reaches of mountain country in the U.S. states and territories.

The men enjoyed the enforced leisure, giving them a chance to drink and gamble their danger-won gains away. Also the black-eyed *senoritas* were obliging. But Sam Vano always chafed restlessly under his own steely restraints. During the long months that followed, he'd learned that Texas Ranger patrols were watching the border for his return. Only when the Rangers had relaxed their vigilance had Vano moved.

During the weeks they'd ridden north; in the saddle by night and holing up by day in the more populated country, the leader gave the others no hint of his plans. Johnny knew only that a fat letter, date marked two months earlier in Rutherford, Wyoming, and frayed and dog-eared from many miles of different hands, had been delivered to Sam a week before they started north. But that was Sam's standing policy: keep them in ignorance of a job till the last minute so no one would have time to crawfish out.

Now, with his first touch of jubilance in many months, Vano grunted, "Bowie, it was worth it. You'll see." His eyes—bullet-gray, with a bullet's impact—moved over the others, then fell to the ground between his feet. He picked up a charred twig from the crumbling embers and began to sketch in the dirt. "This's the Little Muddy River, which we crossed this mornin'. It takes a wide bend around the hills here, and circles the town of Rutherford, just west of where we are now.

This town supplies ranchers for a big area. Been a prosperous year for those ranches. Exceptional spring round-up. Town's got one bank. It's still loaded with local cattlemen's stock income." He looked at them, man by man, and said flatly: "We're taking it."

Bowie started to speak, but his words dissolved in a raw, retching cough. When the spasm ended, he got out breathlessly, "How you know all this? You ain't had time to size up the layout."

Sam Vano reached in his shirt and drew out the thick letter which Johnny had just glimpsed back in Sonora—now more grimy and dog-eared than ever. "This here letter's from Mort Huggins. You remember Mort."

Johnny remembered Mort Huggins—a cadaverous-looking outlaw who'd joined briefly with the gang in the Tonto Rim country about three years ago. Bowie nodded. "Good man, Mort."

Vano read the letter aloud, frowning and stumbling over the tersely-phrased scrawl. Mort had written that he'd been contacted by a young clerk in the Rutherford bank—Emmett Gorman by name—who had been losing heavily at faro in a local gaming room, to the tune of nearly two thousand dollars. The dealer held his I.O.U.'s for the entire sum. Gorman had succeeded in wheedling off payments for six months, promising to pay in full at the end of that time.

20

At first he'd had the idea of embezzling that amount by minor degrees from his own teller's cage, but a shortage couldn't be covered indefinitely, and a full investigation would eventually find him out. He had to find a way to cover the loss. So he looked up Mort Huggins and made him a proposal. It was well-known that Mort rode on the shady side of the law, but there were no warrants out for him at present, and he was keeping to the open.

Gorman's proposition was this: he would give Mort Huggins the complete layout of the bank, including the combination to the big vault and any other pertinent information. The day before Mort pulled the job, Gorman would quietly remove two thousand dollars from the vault—a loss that would be assumed by bank officials to be part of the holdup loot. It was a tempting offer, but Mort refused, telling Gorman that it would take at least four men to pull a sure-fire daytime bank job in a town of Rutherford's size. Besides, the sheriff of Rutherford County was Leonard Wolfe, one of the shrewdest and most relentless lawmen in the territory, and Mort wanted no truck with him.

However, Mort Huggins had made Gorman a counter offer: one that would involve no personal risk for Mort. His friend Sam Vano enjoyed a calculated risk. Sam and his gang were in Sonora, last Mort had heard, but for five hundred dollars he'd contact Sam and put it up to him. Gorman agreed to remove enough from the vault to cover Mort's fee, if Mort were willing to wait. He was and he lost no time in composing the lengthy letter to Sam.

Mort added that he intended to leave for up north so he wouldn't be connected with the job. Later on, he'd return to collect his five hundred. Therefore Sam was not to waste time trying to contact Mort when he reached Rutherford, but to get directly in touch with the bank clerk, who would give them all the necessary details to bring off a smooth job. Gorman lived in a room at the hotel.

"That's the story Mort gave me, I liked the sound of it, and here we are," Sam Vano concluded, folding the letter between his scarred, stubby fingers.

"Here we are," echoed Bowie, dryly. "It occurs to you this could be a law trap?"

Sam Vano gave his spare, humorless side-flick of a smile. "Ain't but a chance in a thousand a square lad like Mort would side with the law to get Sam Vano in a jackpot."

Lopez, legs scissored under him tailor-fashion, leaned forward, mahogany-sphinx face polished by firelight. "W'at about thees *Senor* Gorman. Could not he, how you say, string along the Mort Huggins?"

"Use Mort to toll us into a trap? Maybe," Vano

grunted, "but you been with Sam Vano a while longer, Chino, you'll learn he rides into nothing blind." His lead-gray eyes moved to Jesse, then to Johnny. "That's why you two roosters are going to handle the spadework for this job."

Bowie groaned, started to object, but a lift of Sam's hand cut him off. "You boys will ride into town, register at the hotel. If anyone asks, you're trail hands from Texas, just finished a drive from Montana, and are headin' back. You'll see Gorman on the quiet. That's important. Ask him questions, get all the dirt we need. You'll ride out of town in the morning—south toward Texas, in case anyone sees you go—then swing back and meet us here. Now—Bowie?"

"I was goin' to suggest," Bowie said sourly, "that you send just one man, a more experienced head. Like me. There's bad blood between these two; they might tip our hand with their private feud."

"That's why I'm sendin' 'em," Vano said, his eyes very flat and hard on Jesse and Johnny. "Time they had more know-how, plannin' and organizin'. Also to learn to keep their spurs tucked in. Can't have this personal grudge stuff in the gang. In Rutherford, they'll have to get along or dig their own graves. But they'll dig 'em without the rest of us."

Both boys stared sullenly at the fire. For a moment there was a ponderous silence broken only by the thin moan of wind through leafy oak branches, as Sam let his statement sink home.

"All right," Bowie said mildly. "But what about this Wolfe? I've heard of him; he's smart and tough as they come, no jackleg John Law. He's like to spot these two greenhorns."

Sam was already shaking his head. "That's just it. Wolfe's an old-time lawman, likely to spot a pair of old hardcase birds like you or me right off. Fact, he knows my face from long ago, back in Texas. These two smooth-faced young 'uns would stand a better chance of passin' with Lenny Wolfe, posin' as a pair of lone riders."

"Long riders, don't you mean?" growled Bowie. He drew his shoulders in, shivering in spite of the fire's roasting aura.

"Quit worryin'," Sam said irritably. "Swear, you're gettin' worse than an old squaw."

"Can't help it. Got a bad feeling about this job . . . that's all."

Jesse cleared his throat. "When you want us to ride to town, Uncle Sam?"

Sam swung his gaze to Jesse, curtly answering his question: "Tonight."

CHAPTER THREE

Following Sam Vano's directions, Johnny and Jesse rode due northwest through the foothills, full gear on their saddle to heighten the impression of two drifting cowhands. Sam had known this country from years ago, and his mental mapping was flawless. In fifteen minutes, as he'd predicted, the two young men hit a wagon road. This they followed due west through rugged pine timber till they came out on a denuded ridge. Here they paused to blow their horses and listen to thunder rumble thinly across the peaks to the north.

"More rotten-mean weather coming," Jesse commented sourly. Johnny didn't answer. He'd resolved to say nothing to Jesse that didn't need saying; they couldn't afford a quarrel on a crucial mission. But Jesse himself appeared to be taking this seriously; unusual for him, he'd hardly spoken since leaving camp. Johnny peered through the darkness at Jesse's slim silhouette, slack-easy in the saddle, wishing he could see his cousin's face. Somehow his very silence made Johnny uneasy. Of what was he thinking? The job ahead? Or was he still brooding on how Sam had knocked him down, hating in silence like an Indian?

They took their way along a right forking of the road, following the ridge south for five miles. They descended into a dip where the main tributary of the Little Muddy roiled tumultuously, swollen by the day's heavy rain. Crossing a rickety bridge, they rode down a densely timbered slope and broke at last into the open flat between the hills where the town of Rutherford sprawled.

It was plain that Rutherford was no ordinary backwoods cowtown. On the outskirts they rode through a substantial residential section of big, prosperous-looking houses with rambling verandas and gingerbread trim. The streets were bordered with hedges, picket fences, and giant shade trees. Johnny felt a hungry resurgence of the old yearnings as his eyes eagerly took in the comfortable homes with their warm sprinkling of window lights. Once he glimpsed a couple standing in the shadows of a broad veranda, and a girl's spritely laugh carried clearly.

The subdued mutter of thunder was louder now. It began to rain again as they turned down into the mud-rutted main street. Doors and windows were all closed, except for one open doorway where a bulky figure leaned. A tortured rope of lightning writhed across the sky, bathing the buildings in burnished white. Just then Johnny was looking at the man in the doorway; the flickering light picked out his face, staring straight at the two riders, and above his head, a lettered sign: *Sheriff's Office.*

They rode on. Johnny heard Jesse's breath release sharply. "So that's him. He *is* a watchful bastard."

"And he was watchin' us."

"Don't start cryin' before you been bit, tiger," Jesse gibed. "Hell, he can't know us."

They rode to the livery barn and stabled their horses, asked for and received permission to leave their saddle gear there, then slogged through mud and pelting rain to the hotel, a two-storied sturdy building with the legend *ROOMS* over the entrance nearly weathered away. The dimly lighted lobby was deserted except for the night clerk and a drummer snoring in a plushy leather chair, a newspaper over his face.

Jesse and Johnny registered under the false names that Sam Vano had directed them to use. With a bare glance at their rough-printed signatures, the night clerk selected a key from the wall rack. "Number 102, gentlemen. Second floor, second room to your right. That'll be a dollar apiece in advance."

Johnny was unbuttoning his slicker to reach his wallet when Jesse nudged him in the ribs and jerked his head at the door. "Checking on us already," he murmured.

The bulky man had just pushed through the

27

door and was crossing the lobby, heavy body rolling from side to side with his lumbering walk.

"If anything happens now, he'll know our faces," Johnny whispered.

"Keep your mouth shut," Jesse murmured. "I'll handle this."

The sheriff came to the desk, his shabby, rain-spotted coat stretching taut across his wide shoulders as he hunched over to scan the register. There was a deceptive aspect of a sleepy, shaggy bear about him. The cloudy ruff of sparse light hair around his big head gave an impression of tired benevolence as did the half-lidded pale blue eyes that now swung on the two young men.

"Evenin'," Jesse said, with a civil bob of his head. "Night for ducks, eh?"

"Evenin'." The sheriff's drawl was deep-chested and booming. "Pete Lacy and Tom Brooks of Valverde, Texas, eh?"

"That's right, sir. I'm Pete, this's Tom. Just drove a feeder herd clear to Montana, headin' home now."

"Leonard Wolfe." The sheriff shook hands with both. "What part of Montana?"

"Northwest corner."

"Mmp. Reckon you Texas boys felt right at home on all that rollin' prairie."

"No, sir," Jesse said glibly. "That part's near

solid timber—yellow pine, white pine, fir, hemlock. Some hilly grazing land. Mighty pretty country."

"My mistake. Staying over to see the elephant?"

"Gettin' an early start south in the mornin', sir."

A curt nod of Wolfe's heavy head. "Pleasant trip." He said to the clerk, "Night, Bill," and left the lobby at his tired bear roll of a walk.

Jesse slapped a silver cartwheel on the desk. "Suspicious law hereabouts."

"Keeps his eyes open is all, stranger," the clerk said. "That's why he's one of the best, even at sixty-two."

They ascended the creaking stairway to a narrow, dirty corridor. Jesse unlocked their door and stepped into the room with Johnny following. Jesse dug out a match, lighted the lamp on the dresser. It was a meagerly furnished cubbyhole with a battered commode, an iron bedstead with most of the paint flaked off, a chair which would never take a man's weight, and a cracked pitcher and basin.

Jesse flung his hat on the bed with an explosive laugh. "The clever bastard! Trying to catch us with that Montana business. Good thing we holed up in them woods a couple winters ago."

"After the hold-up, he'll remember our faces," Johnny said.

Jesse shrugged out of his slicker with a disgusted sound. "Hell, knock off that tack.

Chances you take are part of the game." He flopped on his back across the sagging bedframe, grunted luxuriously, and tilted his hat over his eyes.

"We better see Gorman right now," Johnny said.

Jesse groaned, swung his long body to a sitting position, and ran his hands over his hair. "Hell. What room did Mort's letter say?"

Johnny shucked off his slicker and tossed it across the chair. "One-oh-four. Two doors down."

They eased quietly from the room and moved on tiptoe to 104. A pencil of light flowed from the crack beneath the door. Jesse tapped his knuckles softly on a panel. A chair scraped back in the room, and the door opened. A sandy-haired, balding and bespectacled young man stood blinking at them. He wore a black suit of old-fashioned cut. In muted lampglow, his face looked sallow. There was a nervous tic in his left cheek.

"Well?"

"You Gorman?"

"Who are you?"

"You want a bank robbed or not?" Jesse asked amusedly.

The young man's jaw sagged. "You're Sam Vano?"

Jesse prodded a thumb against Gorman's stocky chest and moved him gently backward. "Let's talk inside."

Gorman bolted the door behind them with feverish haste. Jesse swung the single chair around, straddled it, settled his arms on its backrest, and watched Gorman's nervous precautions with a deepening amusement. "I'm Sam's nephew, Jesse Norcross. Sam's son here, 'Tiger' Vano. Sit down, fella, before you fall down."

Johnny put his back to the wall, folded his arms, and watched Gorman sink onto the edge of the bed, twisting his hands like a pair of damp spiders. Johnny guessed at the measureless strain under which the clerk had labored: it could tear the guts out of man.

Emmett Gorman took a folded paper from an inside pocket of his coat and handed it to Jesse. "Here's a floor plan of the bank. What else do you want?"

Sam had rehearsed them both to the letter on the information he needed, but Johnny let Jesse do the talking, and Jesse was thorough. Consulting the floor plan pressed smooth on his knee, he grunted off terse questions about what hours the bank's business was slackest, which employees were likely to play heroic, and so on. Finally, tucking the plan in his pocket, Jesse stood up, yawned, and gave Emmett Gorman a cheerful nod. "Real thorough, Mr. Gorman. You'd have made a hell of an owlhoot."

Gorman stood too, round eyes feverishly eager

behind the thick glasses. "Tomorrow morning, then? The job, I mean? I'll need time to get my money from the vault before you come."

"Likely. But Sam'll set the time." Jesse chuckled.

"What's that for?"

"Just thinking. I never saw dollar signs in a man's eyes before."

Ruddy rage beat through Gorman's face; he took a step toward Jesse, his hands knuckling into fists.

"Don't get feisty, prissy Alice, or I'll pull your pigtails," Jesse drawled, as he lounged toward the door. He shot back the bolt, opened it a crack and surveyed the corridor. He looked back at Gorman. "One little thing, counter-jumper. The total head money on Sam and the rest of us comes to maybe five thousand dollars."

Gorman stared at him with undiluted hatred. "What's that to do with me?"

"Only this," Jesse said gently. "That's considerable more than you'd planned on taking out of this. Tip off the sheriff, and you stand to collect a lot more, *inside* the law—with a ready-sounding excuse for your own part. So tie to this: if anything goes wrong tomorrow, even five thousand won't help you run far enough."

He nodded to Johnny and the two returned to their room. When Johnny had closed the door after them, he turned to Jesse hotly: "That was smart, putting it in his head about the reward money!"

Jesse was sitting on the bed, tugging off his boots. He said easily, "Just a word of warning to the man, tiger. He's hungry, you noticed, real hungry." He laughed. "Fancy that mousy runt running up a two thousand dollar gambling debt . . . just goes to show you can't tell about some folks." He rolled onto the bed and lay with his back to Johnny, saying unconcernedly, "Blow out that damn' lamp and let's get some sleep."

Johnny glared at his back, then deliberately stripped off his shirt, poured some water into the basin, and began to sponge off his bony upper body. He stared at himself in a shard of cracked mirror held by bent nails to the wall over the commode. His rib-lean body, narrow as a lath. His young face, sunblackened and gaunt-angled, his straight hair bleached past its natural blondness. The wariness of a man on the dodge showed in his deep-set amber eyes, making them older than his years warranted. *What're you looking for?* he asked the image silently. *What the hell you expect to find, anyhow?*

Over on the bed, Jesse stirred, grunted impatiently. "You hear me about the lamp?" Johnny toweled himself dry, blew out the lamp, pulled off his boots and rolled in, back to Jesse.

Rain rattled against the window. The lower

sash was open a crack; a rain-scented draft fingered the dry, musty air of the room. A woman's raucous laugh drifted downstreet from a saloon or crib-house, carrying with it a lifetime's disillusionment. It was a familiar sound. Johnny thought of the buoyant, life-loving laugh of that girl in the shadows of the big house, coming into town. The bitter frustration came back to him.

Jesse's sleepy voice startled him. "Caught the way you pulled that hogleg on me, back in camp. Faster even than Sam."

Johnny didn't reply. He folded his arms behind his head and stared ceilingward, at darkness, at nothing.

"Yessir, you're gettin' to be some shucks, tiger," Jesse murmured sleepily. "Only you want to counterweight that butt so's the barrel won't throw so hard. Next time you might not be lucky enough to brace me while I'm flat on my back."

CHAPTER FOUR

The bad weather had not lifted by morning. Johnny and Jesse woke to a gray and dismal dawning, checked out of the hotel, and claimed horses and gear at the livery barn. Mist hung in the air like a thin, wet powder, sleekly burnishing slickers and horses' hides. As they rode past the sheriff's office, Johnny saw Wolfe watching them through the single dingy window. Jesse gave the sheriff an audacious salute of parting, and Wolfe replied with a curt nod.

"Now," Jesse chuckled, "we'll head south on the wagon road like a couple of cowpokes moseying back to Texas, then cut off and circle 'round back to camp."

A mile from town, they loped off from the road, cutting at right angles into thick timber. Then they sloped in a wide circle through deep hills.

Sam received Gorman's map from Jesse and scrutinized it while he rattled questions at the two. When he was satisfied, the leader said, "Pay attention now, all of you."

With a twig, Sam sketched on the wet ground in the lee of the big rock. Working only from his knowledge of the country and his memory of

Rutherford's layout, he made lines and squares to represent two streets and key buildings. He drew the wavering course of the Little Muddy, and worked in lesser streams and tributaries. He drew in roads and locations of prominent landmarks. While he sketched, he talked, naming or describing these matters in detail. He timed and placed each separate movement of each man, from where they'd leave the horses and who would hold them to which roads each would travel—for the gang would separate and scatter after the job, then converge on a single rendezvous later: another of Sam Vano's personal earmarks for confusing pursuit. They'd hole up in rough country for a couple of weeks till the searching posses were discouraged, then travel out of the country by easy stages.

Sam went over it three times, then rapid-fired questions at them to make sure each man was thoroughly briefed on his part. Afterward they dispersed to break camp.

The five men rode in silence, dark-slickered forms without identity in the slanting rain. Occupied with his thoughts, feeling nothing but the beating water against hat and slicker, Johnny rocked emptily with the motion of his horse. He hardly glanced up till Sam Vano said curtly, "Hold it."

Johnny saw buildings take dim shape through

the storm. They'd reached the outfringe of Rutherford. "String out," Sam told them. "We'll ride in one by one and go into the bank together. Bowie, you'll watch the horses—and Lenny Wolfe's office. Have your saddle gun ready. Plug him if he steps out."

Bowie said nothing. No great shakes with a hand-gun, he was the best rifle shot in the gang. Only Johnny, and maybe Sam, guessed how this life had begun to pall on him with encroachment of death in his shriveling body.

"You hear me, Bowie?"

"I hear you, Sam."

"I'll go first," Vano said. "Bowie next, rest of you follow. Time it a minute apart."

Sam spurred away, slowed as he neared the first building, and finally vanished down a residential street. They sat in the rain, waiting without talk. Bowie dipped a scrawny hand inside his slicker and took out his big turnip watch, consulting it more as a gesture than anything. "Luck, boys," he said, and kicked his horse into motion.

"Your turn, tiger," Jesse said in a faintly jeering voice.

Johnny hesitated, needled by something in Jesse's tone, by Bowie's communicated reluctance, by his own uneasiness. Then he heeled his sorrel hard, heading into the side street.

He turned onto the main street at the

intersection and hauled in his fiddlefooting animal, then peered through the wet murk toward the bank, a block down. There were Sam and Bowie on the sidewalk, their horses tied at the front rack. Johnny's gaze raked along the tie rails opposite the bank, at the saddle horses standing hipshot there, wet rumps shimmering softly in the rain. An unusual number of people in town, considering the weather . . . Johnny took passing notice of this, then roweled the sorrel downstreet.

As he swung down, ducked under the tie rail, and moved up on the walk by Sam and Bowie, Johnny realized that Bowie was arguing quietly and that Sam was nodding in agreement. The leader's bleak eyes threw darting restless glances up and down the street. "Maybe you're right," he murmured. "I must need spectacles. Too damn' many horses . . ."

"There," Bowie said quickly, nodding toward the hotel diagonally across from the bank, and Johnny caught it too—a swift flicker of movement behind a second-story hotel window. "Know what?" Bowie asked softly. "Bet you there's men watching us from each of those windows across the way."

"Won't give you odds," Sam Vano said impassively, and Johnny, in a swift grip of panic, made an impulsive step toward the horses. Sam's steely fingers caught his upper arm with bruising power. "Easy, boy. They'd cut us down like flies, in the street. We'll break when I give the word. . . . Here comes Lopez. Wait'll we're all together, we'll make a rush for that alley alongside the bank. We'll take to the timber."

"On foot? They'll ride us down in no time," Bowie prophesied grimly.

"I know this country," Vano said. "I know places no horse can follow. They come after us, they'll have to do it on our terms."

Now Lopez had reached the tie rail. The half-breed dismounted and began to step around his horse. Suddenly a man in town clothes burgeoned out the hotel door. Johnny saw him swing a shotgun to level, pull both triggers. The double blast bucketed racketing echoes down the street. It caught Lopez just as he stepped into view from behind the horse's flank, flinging him backward, rolling him into the hoof-churned mud where he sprawled like a broken rag doll.

Buck fever took Johnny by the throat and shook him; for a moment, his brain refused to function. Sam Vano dropped to one knee, blazing away at the townsman. The fellow dropped his shotgun, reeled away, clawing at the clapboard siding of the hotel, and fell in a sodden sprawl across the board walk.

It was the signal for the men in the windows to open up. Bullets gouted chocolate geysers in the muddy thoroughfare, ripped in screaming ricochets off the brick front of the bank. *"Run for it!"* Sam Vano bellowed, leaping for the alleyway. Bowie took a step after him, then saw Johnny frozen there.

"Johnny-boy, come on!" His clawing grip tore at Johnny's slicker, tugged him into a stumbling run. He heard the impact of lead thudding into flesh, heard Bowie's retching, lung-torn gasp, felt Bowie's falling weight tear away his hold on Johnny's arm.

"Bowie!" It shocked Johnny to life. He dropped on his knees by Bowie. Sam glanced at Bowie's gray face, said sharply, "He's cashed, kid. Let's grab our horses, ride through these soft-bellied counterjumpers, pick Jesse up as we head out. . . ."

While he was still speaking, Sam had grabbed Johnny by the shoulder, half-lifting him, hauling him in a dragging run under the tie rail, clamping Johnny's hand over his stirrup before he swung to his own horse. The feel of the stirrup was enough to galvanize Johnny's tense-tight muscles to the automatic reflex of mounting. As he hit the saddle swell, a bullet smashed the horn, another whipped the skirt of his slicker. The townsmen were rattled and shooting wild. Johnny quartered around and spurred headlong after Sam.

The gamut of gunfire fell behind them. *We're making it,* Johnny was thinking, when a man appeared in a doorway to fire at the passing riders. Sam Vano's oxlike form rocked to the impact of a bullet. Seemingly it was a minor graze, for Sam instantly twisted in his saddle without cutting pace and returned the fire. The man spun under a shoulder hit and staggered into the shop. Then they veered around the block, up the side street, a corner building cutting them off from random fire.

"Now ride like hell!" Sam grated. "That's why they had them horses ready, case any slipped out of the ambush. . . ."

Wind whipped at Johnny's face, tearing his words away. "Jesse? Where is he?"

"Must've cut and run when he heard the shooting."

The town began to fall behind. Only a few outskirt houses remained before the street petered out on the twisting wagon road. Johnny, squinting and blinking at the pouring rain, didn't at first react to the sight of a barely seen figure running out through a picket gate into the street.

"Daddy?" It was the frightened voice of a small girl. That was all that Johnny knew, except that he was frantically reining in his horse, yelling thinly, "Sam, the kid, look—"

Sam Vano didn't slacken his headlong pace, didn't pull aside. Johnny saw the big black pound past the small, crumpled form.

Johnny quartered his horse around, body

41

tensing to swing down, when a door opened beyond the picket gate. A woman's scream knifed the lashing storm.

Johnny drove in his spurs; his horse reared, bolted after the black. Sobs tore his chest as he quirted the animal with his reins, savagely, viciously, and not caring.

CHAPTER FIVE

They lined onto the wagon road, rolling ahead of them like a dark brown ribbon. Johnny was just behind Sam Vano, the leader's broad, slickered back filling his blurred vision. *He must have seen that little girl,* Johnny's thoughts ran numbly. *I did. But he rode right over her like he didn't hear me—or didn't give a damn. Only maybe he didn't see her, coming on top of her that way, maybe he couldn't hear me for the damned wind—*

Sam was slowing to a trot, his granite-etched face turning to Johnny as he swung his arm around toward a high ridge shouldering away to their left. "We'll cut off, head up there. Won't be looking for us to leave the road till we're well away, figurin' we'd put plenty of fast distance between town an' us."

They pushed their horses into a plunging, stumbling lunge up the long boulder-strewn incline.

Soon a posse of men poured around the bend that cut off their view of the town. At least thirty men. The roar of churning hoofs diminished in the wailing storm, and they were gone.

Johnny glanced at Sam. Vano's hatbrim

whipped suddenly back in a wind-driven gust, and Johnny saw the stony face beneath white and strained in a vivid flare of lightning. Sam began to bow forward across his pommel, his weight sloughing sideways. Then his lax hands clenched into fists over the horn and held him in the seat. *More than a graze,* Johnny thought in panic: he was hard-hit.

Johnny half-fell out of the saddle to reach Sam's side. The slate eyes stared dully into his. "All right, kid. You'll have to get us both out of this." The effort to speak cost him an agonizingly drawn breath; for a moment he gulped air, then pulled erect, calling on some untapped reserve of iron vitality. "You take my reins, I'll direct you to a place I know of . . . never find us there . . ."

It was a nightmarish journey for Johnny. He plodded through sheets of falling water that drove in solid masses against face and body as though to smash him back, to drown him. When he looked over his shoulder, Sam Vano's bulk was only a spectral shape rocking back and forth; his reins clutched in Johnny's half-frozen fist the only thing connecting them in the storm's fury.

"East . . . high stony bluff . . ." was all Vano had gasped before he lapsed into a half-coma; only a superhuman effort of will keeping him in the saddle. All Johnny could do was hold to a due southerly route in the teeth of the raging

elements. If there was one bright spot, it was this: not even an Indian could trail them after this storm.

Johnny came upon the bluff and then worked south till he found what he sought: a shallow cave eroded into the base rock and nearly concealed by a tangle of low-growing brush. Johnny dismounted and hobbled at a cramped and stiff-legged gait to the mouth. He had to crouch low and worm through the brush to get inside. He found the cave dry and spacious, though so low-roofed he was obliged to bend almost double. Thanks to the dense foliage crowding the mouth, a man could spot anyone sneaking up long before they could be sure of his position.

He returned to the horses and led them to a brushy covert close to the wall, where the high liprock would also afford some shelter. He ground-hitched the animals there. Sam was almost wholly unconscious now; he didn't respond by a twitch to Johnny's voice or tugging hands. It took all Johnny's strength to unpry the leader's death-grip on the horn. As Sam's limp hulk toppled sideways, Johnny braced himself and somehow kept his feet as he caught Sam's full weight and eased it to the ground. He tried to lift the leader across his shoulders and, in his own sluggish exhaustion, failed. Finally he grabbed Sam under the arms and dragged him across the stony ground into the cave. Then he lugged their saddles and gear inside.

Sam's tough hide had been scored with a good deal of lead in a lifetime; he still carried some of it. But the leader's bluing lips and shallow breathing told him that this time Sam Vano had crossed the narrow margin between life and death: an ordinary man would be dead by now.

The first raw shock of realization left Johnny oddly steady. He tore up a fairly clean shirt he found stuffed inside Sam's blankets and made a fresh compress and bandages. He tied the wound tightly and wrapped the unconscious man in his blankets. He couldn't afford to think of what this would mean, he had to keep his hands and thoughts occupied. He left the cave and scoured up some dry dead brush. He built a small fire that made a clean, smokeless blaze in the mouth of the cave, and crouched over its warmth, palms extended, to thaw his chilled, soaked body. Then he took off his clothes and propped them on sticks near the fire, afterward wrapping himself in a blanket and settling down with his back to the rough wall and his gun in his fist.

He dozed on and off through the remaining hours of daylight, jerking to wakefulness at every least sound and scrambling to the entrance to stare out at empty, rain-lashed distance, though he knew there was only the barest chance that even an organized posse would find them while the storm lasted. Probably the searchers had long since broken up and returned to town.

When some of his jitters had worn off, he relaxed at last into full sleep only to be brought out of it by Sam's voice. The leader was awake, his gray stare clear-eyed and rational on Johnny. "Made it, eh? I'd like a drink."

Johnny was reaching for a canteen when Sam said dryly, "There's a pint of J. H. Cutter in my saddlebag," and when Johnny hesitated, he rapped harshly, "Give it here!"

Johnny dug out a half-empty bottle of whiskey and silently handed it to him. Vano gulped most of the remaining contents before he leaned back, gasping, and told Johnny flatly, "Finish it. You need the heat."

Johnny choked on his first raw swallow, but drained the bottle. A stove-like glow spread through his belly.

"Reckon we both know it's up with me," Sam said calmly. Johnny said nothing. Vano's rock-hewn face didn't alter as he went on, "That little kid—"

Johnny's head lifted swiftly. "You saw her?" Something constricted in his chest like a closing fist.

Vano's thin lips twitched. A thing close to emotion shaded his opaque eyes. "Funny thing," he mused. "A man spends a lifetime killing, robbing, it never touches him. Things was always black or white to me, no grays, no shadings. I was always a funny owlhoot that way, went into it with my eyes open. Just never gave a damn. Liked doing it, was all. But this mornin', when I saw that kid run in front of me and didn't bother to pull aside—" He shook his shaggy head, let it bow on his chest. "Funny. That six-gun of mine must have orphaned a dozen kids and it never meant anything. But that little girl keeps coming back. All the way here, I was rockin' out of my head in the saddle, and her ridin' with me every foot of the way . . ."

"Sam—"

"Let me talk, kid. Haven't much longer. Things you have to know. I'm bad, bad all through. Always knew it, but it never got me till now . . ." He lifted his head, glaring feverishly at Johnny. "You hate this life. Bowie saw it, and he wanted you to clear out. I saw it, and was too twisted up inside to give a damn. Bowie was right, kid . . . get out of it."

"Get out of it," Johnny echoed bitterly. "Just like that. Who was it always told me there was no turnin' back?"

Sam stirred an impatient hand beneath the blanket. "Lots worse characters than you started over clean. Your name's known to the law, but not your face."

"Sheriff Wolfe knows it—after last night."

"He can't connect it to you, though, not unless

he got a good look at you today, and that ain't likely . . . If you don't want to risk a fresh start in the states, there's Canada, South America, even Europe. Man can work his way before the mast." His hand shot out, caught Johnny's wrist, fevered eyes yellow-tinged in the firelight. "You go straight from here on. Promise!"

"You're my father," Johnny yelled, his eyes suddenly smarting. "All my life you pulled me your way. Top of that, I'm your blood. Supposin' I want to, how can I change things now?"

"Because you want to," Vano said harshly. "That's all you need. Me, I don't know if there's anythin' to this business of bad blood runnin' in a family. My folks was strait-laced Ohio farmers. Other hand, my sister turned out no good, Jesse's her boy, he's pure coyote. But this don't apply to you." He fell back in his blankets, hauling stertorous breaths. "You ain't my son, Johnny."

Johnny watched him numbly.

"There was a Ute massacre of an emigrant train just below the Canadian River, twenty years ago. My gang and me came on it a day after, found a toddler bawling in the sage near a wrecked wagon. Injuns missed you. You must of walked out of the wagon after it was over. It was Bowie's crazy idea that we raise you, and I agreed if we'd pass you as my son. I had some fool notion that a son would be useful for taking

49

the reins when I got too old to handle the men. I raised you tough and mean to that end."

"My people," Johnny said huskily.

"All gone, wiped out, whoever they were."

"Don't matter where I came from," Johnny muttered. "It's what I got to be."

"Listen, you fool kid. I raised you rough as I could and still couldn't stamp out an idea you always had of changing. Difference between a man and an animal is, a man can choose. I know. I chose—wrong. Only thing a man can't choose is bein' born in the first place."

Johnny edged to the mouth of the cave and squatted there, huddled in his blanket. Bright slashing torrents of water cascaded in twinkling streams off the high rimrock and poured past his face in miniature waterfalls. When he spoke, his hunched back to Sam Vano, it was a barely audible mutter. "All right, Sam. I'll try."

Sam Vano grunted, "Good," and closed his eyes. After a while he murmured, "That Gorman bastard, you think?"

Johnny humped his shoulders in a shrug. "Who else? Jesse shot off his mouth in front of Gorman last night about the head money on the Vano gang."

"Damn him," Vano said tonelessly. "Damn that clerk."

"I been thinkin' of doin' more about that," Johnny said in a too-soft tone.

Vano jerked upright, then toppled back with a groan. "Now damn you, listen to me! You got a chance, don't risk it by going after Emmett Gorman."

Johnny had lied: he'd hardly thought through these long hours of Emmett Gorman, but abruptly Gorman gave him a badly needed sense of direction for his own pointless life, for the rage, hate, and frustration that had come to a boil inside him. Thought of revenge on the treacherous clerk provided a relief that was almost overwhelming. So now he lied again: "All right, Sam, just as you say."

"Good boy," Sam Vano mumbled. He was beginning to slip back into semi-consciousness. Shortly afterward, he began raving, about long-ago names and happenings that Johnny had never heard. Finally he fell into a silent, burning fever.

For all that Johnny could do, Sam Vano died before the desolate day had spent itself.

CHAPTER SIX

After dark, the rain stopped at last. A night wind wailed down from the flinty hills, driving the banked storm clouds before it, chilling with a marrow-bite. Johnny left the cave and stepped into a dripping, starlighted evening. He'd made up his mind. Paying back Emmett Gorman's betrayal was something he had to do, even if he used up his last chance.

He tried to tell himself it was because of his three dead fellows, but that didn't ring true. Lopez, a recent addition to the gang, he'd hardly known; the sullen halfbreed had won rapport with no one. The bullet that had blasted away Bowie Samse's life had really been a mercy to a slowly dying man. Sam and Johnny had never been close, and now he'd learned that Sam was not even his father.

True, Sam had given him a chance for life on that long-gone day when he'd picked up a waif survivor of a butchered caravan . . . but what sort of life was this? An endless pilgrimage that kept him one jump ahead of the law . . . with a future of the same stretching drearily ahead. Bowie's and Sam's argument that he could change held no conviction for him; he'd never really believed there was an out beyond his daydreams. Dimly, he understood that this was the real sum of his hatred for Gorman, but he couldn't change the way he felt.

Johnny returned to the cave. With his hands he scooped a shallow trough in the floor and rolled Sam Vano's blanket-wrapped body into it. He filled the grave, then methodically went over Sam's gear for any articles that might be useful. He buried the rest, afterward spreading the sandy floor to pristine smoothness. He stamped out the fire, kicking its smoldering remains into the earth. He dragged dead brush to the cave and piled it across the entrance, obscuring it from a casual observer.

He fetched the horses and threw on his own rig. Then, mounting his own, he quirted Sam's animal, hoorawing it into a run. He sat listening till the sound of hoofbeats died away and turned his horse toward the west, guided by the stars.

He wondered if the sheriff's posses were still combing the countryside. Likely they'd not stay out long while the bad weather held. But tomorrow, if the rain hadn't resumed, they'd be searching for fresh signs of the fugitives. Jesse had doubtlessly made a clean getaway, and was well out of the area by this time. *And you'd be smart to do the same,* he told himself, knowing he wouldn't, though. An old fox like Wolfe would have the roads covered. He'd have his posses organized into far-flung, yet close-knit cordons that a rabbit couldn't break through. And he could send word to other towns in his district, telling his deputies to assemble search parties to head off the fugitives.

He rubbed his palm across the thin, youthful rasp of his week-old beard. How to reach Gorman? Why not play it bold and open? The citizenry might be keyed-up enough, after the morning's excitement, to shoot at a skulking figure, but not at a casually incoming stranger. They'd never conceive of a bank robber crazy enough to ride back into a town which had driven him out in a hail of gunfire.

When he passed the sheriff's office, he let out a held breath when he saw the darkened window. Dogged, tireless lawman that he was, Wolfe was still out scouring the hills where the robbers would be likely to hole up. He dismounted by the hotel, tied his horse, and sent a roving glance up and down the street before moving to a lobby window. The same clerk who'd been on duty last night was dozing in his chair behind the desk. *Suppose he was in that deadfall this morning and saw my face?* Johnny thought warily. Unlikely, though, that anyone had caught more than a distant, fleeting glimpse of him . . .

Johnny opened the door and stepped quietly

inside, hoping to make the stairs without waking the clerk, but the man came instantly awake as the door opened. Johnny crossed the lobby to the desk, casually brushing raindrops from his slicker. "Evenin'."

"Hoddy." The clerk stood, yawning, giving him an idle once-over, and some of the tension left Johnny. "Say, ain't you one of the fellas was going to Texas?"

"Uh-huh. My pard went on, I decided to stay awhile. Rode around the country today, like the looks of it."

"Oh." The clerk's bored gaze sharpened. "Say, you meet any of the posses on the road?"

"Posses?"

"That's right, you rode out this mornin' early, hell, they was a lot of excitement later on . . . Sam Vano gang rode in this mornin' to hit the bank. Lenny Wolfe had an ambush rigged, got two. He's out lookin' for the others."

Johnny whistled softly. "Vano, eh? No, I didn't meet nobody. I hung to the road most of the time; reckon they'd hit for the deep brush."

"Reckon. Everyone in town, just about, joined the search. Bastards rode down a little kid, Jenny Carpentier, when they left. Got the town madder'n a nest of riled hornets."

Johnny's heart thudded almost to a stop. "Kid bad hurt?"

The clerk spread his pale hands. "Ain't sure

she'll pull through, that's all I heard. You want a room?"

Johnny said yes, signed "Tom Brooks" to the register, gave the clerk a dollar, received his key, and tramped up the shabbily-carpeted staircase. He'd wanted to ask the clerk if he knew who'd tipped off the sheriff about the robbery, except that might stretch a successful bluff too far. *Hell,* he thought, *you know who . . .*

At the head of the stairs, he paused in the gloom to unbutton his slicker. He slipped his .45 from its holster, checked the loads, and moved on tiptoe to Gorman's door. A board creaked under the boot, and he stiffened. He could hear the pen scratching on paper in the room—and now it stopped. Realizing that Gorman had probably bolted the door, Johnny thought fast, then spoke, imitating the night clerk's high-pitched nasality:

"Message for you."

Gorman's voice cracked with nervousness. "Slide it under the door."

"I'm supposed to get your answer."

He heard Gorman cross the room, heard the bolt shoot back. Johnny wrenched the doorknob and pushed into the room, sending Gorman reeling. Johnny kicked backward, slamming the door, and jammed his gun into the bank clerk's soft belly, doubling him with wheezing pain. "Sit, Gorman."

Emmett Gorman sank into his creaking chair, his face chalky. His eyes jerked uncontrollably. "What do you want?"

"You know what happened today?"

"I had nothing to do with that," Gorman said wildly. "Don't be a young fool, Vano! Why should I—"

"Because it's like Jesse said. You could make more money this way, with no danger to your own rotten hide. The other way, if anything went wrong, if any of us were caught, you knew we wouldn't cover for a rat like you. Five thousand dollars, Gorman . . . blood money you'll never spend. Think about it, because you ain't got long."

The clerk's quivering hulk almost slipped out of the chair. He grabbed for the support of his small writing desk, his whisper a strained gasp. "I swear I didn't breathe a word. Look—look here, I'm in plenty of trouble, I took that money from the vault early this morning, and the robbery didn't come off to cover it. Don't do it, Vano, don't kill an innocent man!"

Unsteady rage dug at Johnny; the gun shook in his fist. "You were ready and willing to cheat your own bank, and you want me to—"

"Yes—because it's the truth!"

Backed to the wall, a coward like Gorman could easily lie with a vehemence that was convincing, Johnny knew—yet he was shaken. *Get it over with before you think about it,* he thought. He cocked the gun and Gorman jerked as though the bullet had already slapped his flesh.

But Johnny's finger never tightened. He knew then that he couldn't do it, and it had nothing to do with Gorman's guilt or innocence. Many things passed through his mind in a breath-hung moment. He'd always had a fatalistic feeling about his blood-tie to Sam Vano, and knew now that it had never existed. That fact was beginning to sink home, leaving him with a curious sense of freedom. Even Sam himself, a cynical hardcase dying in a lonely cave, had been humanized and full of regret. And what had Sam said? *A man has a choice.* And now Johnny Vano, having a choice, meant to shoot a man in cold blood and cement himself for good into a life he hated. . . .

His face showed nothing, and a sick glaze had come over Emmett Gorman's eyes, tensed for the shock of a bullet. Then Johnny holstered the gun, saying quietly, "Don't follow me, Gorman," and turned to the door.

Behind him he heard the clerk's sobbing gasp of relief, but he'd never expected what happened next. He heard Gorman yank open a desk drawer, and he swung quickly around. Goaded by a reaction of rabbity bravado after his sudden reprieve, Gorman had snatched out a nickel-plated .32.

As he swung it to bear, Johnny drew and fired with the reflex of long practice. Gorman buckled at the waist, his white shirt staining red. He stared at Johnny with a sort of stunned reproach, took two steps forward, fell to his knees, and then full length with his face plowing the splintery floor. Johnny stood rooted, hardly believing this. Gorman's outflung hand touched his boot, and he pulled it back quickly. He heard the thunder of feet on the staircase.

Spurred by a dismal urgency, his eyes swung to the open window, curtains bellying inward on the wind. He stepped to it, thrust his head out, seeing the dark gulf of an alleyway beneath. He swung a leg over the sill, then the other. He drew a deep breath and dropped into the darkness just as the door crashed open.

Johnny hit the muddy ground on both feet, but his boots instantly skidded away and flung him on his hip and shoulder. He got his legs under him, driving like pistons. He flung a look over his shoulder as he achieved the mouth of the alley and his waiting horse, and saw the night clerk leaning out the window, mouth opening to yell: "There he is! Get him!" Johnny twisted a backward look, saw the man's gangling figure burgeoning out of the lobby at a jerky run, swinging a pointing finger. There were scattered shots as a few men with six-guns opened up. But they were shooting blind, for Johnny was almost at street's end now, the lighted section behind him, the empty wagon road rolling clear before him.

Then, coming abreast of a darkened doorway, a lone pedestrian, no more than a dark shadow among the shadows, swung up his arm: Johnny caught a gleam of pistol steel. He tried to swerve, to confuse the fellow's aim. The pistol spoke.

A burst of pain knifed through Johnny's left thigh, and he cried out hoarsely and leaned low in the saddle, his face bent into the whipping mane.

CHAPTER SEVEN

Johnny hit the road and lined into a steady, hoof-thrumming pace that was torture to his leg. There had been the first tearing blow, then a numbness that was already receding into rhythmic hammerstrokes of pain. He set his teeth against it, banishing throbbing hurt from his mind. With the icy clarity of a man with his back to the wall, with the savage cunning of a lifetime on the dodge, he assayed his chances. Under the double handicap of a game leg and a fast-tiring horse, he must not only thwart the pursuit from the town that would soon be breathing down his neck, but also break through Wolfe's posse cordons which he now felt certain would be strung out ahead of him.

He reined aside and cut into a skimpy aspen grove bordering the road. He swung down and held his trembling horse, clamping his hand over its nose and mouth. "Quiet, boy . . ." He stood in immobility, listening, not even shrugging in annoyance when a cold dribble from a water-laden branch ran into his collar and down his bare spine. Soon ten or more townsmen thundered past, dark, eager-spurring shapes of fresh, straining mounts.

He stood for another frozen moment as the sound of their going receded down the road. In less than no time they'd have overtaken his faltering horse. In a few more hours it would be light enough to dissipate the off-trail shadows that now concealed him. He must use the remaining darkness to best advantage. . . . He unslung the saddlebags which held his provisions and threw them off. He untied his suggan-roll and let it slide to the ground. Of his saddle gear, he kept only his canteen and rifle. *When you're pressed for your life, don't quibble over shedding trifles,* Sam had always said. *Pound of gear might slow you by just enough.*

In his mind's eye, he reviewed the map Sam had scratched in the dirt nearly twenty-four hours ago (it seemed like years) . . . *Little Muddy River . . . curves around hills mile east of town . . .*

Get lost in unfamiliar country, Sam used to say, *follow the rivers. They'll take you out.* That was an advantage these men had: they knew the country. The river was Johnny's best bet, and water would leave no trail.

He wound a pocket bandanna around his blood-welling thigh, knotting it tightly. That was his greatest fear—that blood loss would slow his reactions and muddy his thoughts to a gray ebb.

He mounted again, then had to hold dizzily to

his pommel for a moment, sickened by the cost of effort to his used-up body. His still-damp clothes were clammy rags against his feverish skin. A cold needle of fear lanced him, alerting to the danger-signs of his waning strength.

He pushed due east, feeling the ground rise beneath him momentarily. He headed up a pine-mantled ridge, into thick timber where a springy needle carpet deadened hoof-falls. He moved through starlight-dappled glades, whose air was pungent with the pitchy pine smell, where the faint soughing of wind in high boughs made a comfortable break in the brooding stillness, thinking how very fine it would be to lie down . . . dream all this away. . . . *Damn that hot poker in his leg.*

The timber ended abruptly in a straggle of stunted trees as he broke onto the western end of the ridge, a bald, exposed promontory. He stopped to blow his horse, feeling the animal's flanks heave like bellows. He would have dismounted and rested except for a cold conviction that if he left the saddle he might not be able to make it back. His leg was stiffening on the chilly air, and his questing hand located the dark wet soaking of his pants: his improvised bandage could not stop the fresh pumping of the wound with each movement of thigh muscles.

Far beyond and below he was aware of a deep rush of sound which he'd at first attributed to the wind. Now, he strained his eyes, finally picking out where a deep, wide gulf bisected his downslope of the ridge. He caught the gleam of water flashing in a silvery torrent, and his heart sank. He would not be riding this river, swollen by rain, even if he could descend the steep walls which confined it.

He blinked his blurring eyes and ran a hand over his wet face. *All right, one way's as good as another. Follow it upstream, maybe it'll widen and shallow out. Maybe . . .*

Shortly the ridge tapered off into low banks. But the water was still too swift and deep, to ride the river bottom, and Johnny had to fight his way through tangles of willow and cherry thickets which choked the banks to the water's edge. Finally in the first gray overcast that hinted at false dawn, he picked out the pale blobs of sandbars, ahead where the river broadened to three times its downstream width. Injected with sudden hope he plunged down the bank, splashed through the shallows toward the nearest sandbar.

Suddenly an orange glow staining the solid black woods not fifty feet to his right and ahead brought him up sharply. A fire . . . *Posse camp,* he thought, wings of panic beating in him. The fire was well-hidden, pocketed in a heavy timber belt: Johnny had spotted it only because he'd come on it from the water instead of the brush-obstructed shore. Wolfe was no fool; he had the river covered, probably at regular points with guards to patrol them. There might be a dozen men lying in concealment almost anywhere. Johnny sat his horse in the shallows, hardly daring to breathe, eyes whipping the thickets and timber along the banks. Cautiously he kneed his horse toward shore, then abruptly kicked it into a lunging climb up the bank. He had to get out of the open, into the timber. . . .

As they topped the bank, a rifle shot sent shattering echoes across the river. It killed the sorrel on its feet; it relaxed in death as it sloughed over sideways with Johnny somehow kicking his bad leg from the stirrup, and rolling free of the falling animal. With an impact that smashed the breath from his lungs, he hit the sloping bank and kept rolling, sliding into the water with a shallow, almost noiseless splash. The misery of the icy river shocked his paralyzed senses to renewed life.

The unseen rifleman shot again, and yet again, but he was firing at shadows now, Johnny knew. He heard the excited voices upstream, and shrank inwardly at Sheriff Wolfe's bull-chested boom, shouting a question.

He let his head sink on his flexed arm in a sick, tired despair, thinking, *Can't dog it any further. Can't run. Can't swim . . . No use trying any more.*

He could see the smoky flare of bobbing torches moving down the bank only yards upstream; the murky water and shadows concealed him now, but they'd be on him in a few minutes. Wearily, he reached out his arm, grabbing for a rough protuberance to drag himself from the water. His hand closed over a dead, barkless limb; as he pulled, a great log attached to the limb rocked with a gurgling sound and slowly settled back.

A new thought jerked life into Johnny's veins; water peeled from his slicker as he staggered to his feet and climbed over the log. He propped the knee of his bad leg against the bank and with the foot of his other leg lunged his whole weight against the huge timber. A wave of flaring pain rippled hotly up his leg. He set his teeth to keep from crying out. The log had stirred. He placed his weight again, shoved, and the log, freed from clogging brush and oozing muck moved out of the shadows.

Johnny waded out, tugging at the massive cylinder of driftwood. It scraped bottom at first, but gained buoyancy as it coasted into deeper water, Johnny finding to his relief that it wasn't waterlogged. The men were so close now he could pick out their words. ". . . swear it came from right here."

Johnny sank prone into the chill water, only his head surfaced, giving the log silent momentum with the drive of his feet against the mucky bottom. Then the bottom fell away in an abrupt drop-off. Johnny, a poor swimmer, grabbed frantically at the log, wrapped his arm around its smooth bole, and hung on as it slid into mid-channel. Suddenly he felt a powerful drag as the mainstream caught the log and swept it along like a cork.

Eddying to left and right, rudderless with the vagaries of the current, the log, with its half-conscious burden, gave itself aimlessly to the river, to the night.

CHAPTER EIGHT

Johnny Vano dreamed he was in hell. He and Sam Vano were squatting on a bed of glowing coals. Sam was wearing a pair of horns and a barbed tail and was saying, *Hell is something folks make up to help 'em keep rules they break anyways.*

But ain't this hell, Sam?

Kid, hell is where a man happens to be. . . .

Johnny groaned and twisted with burning pain. Scenes shifted kaleidoscopically and swam hazily together. And always, at its worst, a cool hand on his head and a woman's voice soothed away the pain till it eased into a vast ocean of peace. That was the part that puzzled him. The girl. Her face was never more than a swimming blur bent over his, and always it receded into the chaotic blur of past memories till he couldn't distinguish reality from nightmare.

Finally, though, he slept. Slept through a long gray interval that was dreamless . . .

When he woke, the girl was there by his bedside. He was in a bed—that startled him. Bright sunlight from an open window checkered the flowered counterpane, and he stared at it for an uncomprehending moment. He remembered an eternity of storm and wetness. No sunlight.

"How long . . . have I been here?" The words husked from his throat in a broken whisper.

He looked at the girl, seeing her eyes widen, her lips part. She was tall, in her late teens, wearing shapeless men's trousers and a hickory shirt which didn't hide the supple lines of her young body. Twin blonde braids were pinned in a coronet around her high-held head; her features were regular, strongly angled, handsome rather than pretty, holding a knowing competence beyond her years.

She touched his forehead. "Fever's down," she murmured.

Johnny felt irritation, despite his lightheaded weakness. What in hell did she think he was, a colt with the colic? "I ain't a baby, lady."

She straightened, rocking on her heels and shoving her hands in her hip pockets. "No? You're as full of questions as a two-year-old, though." She raised her voice. "Mike. Lee. He's awake and sassy."

A man and woman entered the room. Father and his two daughters, Johnny guessed. He warily braced himself for an onslaught of questions as the man moved to the bedside. He was great-framed, slightly stooped, in his early fifties. His graying blonde hair fell in a boyish cowlick over a ruddy, strongly boned Celtic face, gray-rimmed brows frowning over chipped-ice eyes that were clear, bright azure, like the blonde girl's.

He laid a heavy hand on Johnny's shoulder. "Glad to see you poco-poco, boy. You're at my ranch, Tulare. Name's Mike Murphy. My daughter Nan, here, and my wife Leonora."

That was all. No questions, no accusations. Johnny swallowed the knot of panic in his throat, and looked from one to the other. A point of frontier courtesy. Waiting, rather than asking for information. He looked at the tall young woman by the door. Not Murphy's daughter, but his wife. A child-bride, maybe, but she didn't look it. Her skin was soft and pale against the raven mass of hair clubbed at the back of her neck. There was compassion in her face as she regarded Johnny, but its faultless sculpture was accented by an inbred aloofness, marred by a deep shadow of discontent. She wore an expensive dress of watered silk. She didn't fit in with this rough-hewn rancher and his tomboy daughter.

Johnny met Murphy's patient gaze. "Billy Barnes," he said. "Fellow upriver shot me for my poke. Dumped me in the river. All I recall."

Murphy glanced at Johnny's hands on the covers. "Puncher?"

There were plenty of rope-scars on Johnny's

hands—from hazing stolen cattle. "Off and on," he said. "Just drift, mostly."

Boots scraped the floor as a man came swiftly into the room. His clothes were colorless with caked dust; he batted a dusty Stetson against his chaps.

"Boze Hendryx, my foreman," Murphy said. "He's the one hauled you out of the river. Boze, this is Billy Barnes."

Hendryx nodded, drawling, "Hoddy." He was a sparely built man with saddle leather for skin and a long, gaunt face like that of a faithful horse. His jaws, silvered with stubble, clamped on a reeking cob pipe set between his stained teeth. His faded eyes held a kindly, hard-won wisdom that made Johnny uneasy. All of these people made him uneasy; he'd never known their kind. He guessed he hadn't deliriously babbled of his past, for they appeared to accept his story. That was something. But he'd have to watch himself.

"Trouble, cap'n," the foreman said now. "Looks like the Hornes used the bad weather to cover their drivin' off more of your prime whitefaces."

Mike Murphy's face darkened; his hamlike fist lifted. "The Hornes! Those spalpeens. Mountain scum! Wait a bit; I'll change clothes, ride back with you." He gave Johnny a jerky nod, saying curtly, "Boy, get some sleep, get your strength. We'll talk later."

He pivoted on his heel and followed his foreman from the room. Johnny struggled to get his elbows under him. "Look, just fetch me my clothes . . ."

Nan Murphy placed a strong hand on his chest and shoved him back on the pillows. She straightened, setting her fists on her hips, a humorous glint in her eyes. "Look at you. Weak as a cat. Ganted up like a deer-hunting dog. You're not going anywhere, buster. You heard the man. Get some sleep."

The bedridden two weeks that followed laid a heavy tax on Johnny's strength. Then he was giddy and light-headed on his feet. But it was mostly a shaky aftermath of nervous exhaustion; the wound itself, despite blood loss, wasn't too serious, the slug having embedded itself in the outer fleshy muscles of his thigh. A medico from the nearby settlement of Cedar Forks had removed the lead, and healing was quick and clean.

While he mended, Johnny liked loafing around the bunkhouse while the crew was on-range. It was a typical high country bunkroom, with eight sets of double bunks, but the thing that puzzled him was the many unused bunks. The crew now numbered nine men. Despite its prosperous sprawl of labyrinthian barns, sheds and corrals, Tulare ranch was plainly becoming slowly impoverished.

It was Nan Murphy who told him why, while they were sitting on the washbench by the bunkhouse, where she'd joined him. He felt an unspoken pleasure in her company which he couldn't define, for she'd shown him nothing but a cool face and a tart, flippant tongue. He wondered if he'd imagined the gentle care she'd given him when he was sick and out of his head with fever. Johnny Vano knew little of girls, but he sensed that Nan softened toward something only so long as she felt a strong advantage over it.

Just now they were silent, letting their gaze range across the pine-stippled backbones of the foothills. Tulare headquarters was situated on a meadowed slope tucked snugly between two rolling, timbered ridges. The rambling main house, set upslope from the working part of the ranch, was a well-weathered frame building.

The girl broke the silence, nodding toward the purple-heighted scarps to the north. "Pretty, isn't it? Wouldn't think it means ruination for the Murphys, would you?"

"Rustlers?" was Johnny's token reply.

She nodded, an angry edge to her voice: "The Hornes. A bunch of rawhiders from the Ozarks. They squatted on Tulare years ago. Mike ran them off. So they found a valley back in those peaks, a regular walled-in fortress where no one could get at them, and hit our herds off and on, driving small bunches back into the canyons to butcher for beef. About a year ago, someone started heavy, organized raids on our cattle— and they're the logical suspects."

"Gettin' back at your dad, eh?"

"Obviously. They've hardly touched the other ranches, while our cattle are vanishing in droves. The only thing those simple-minded hill folk can remember is a grudge. Feuding is their way of life. But why they suddenly went in for organized cattle-stealing is a puzzle. Where can they market branded beef without bills of sale? How can they drive it to a respected rail outlet without being spotted? The only railhead hereabouts is Rutherford, the county seat, and no cattle thief in his right mind would try to market right under Lenny Wolfe's nose."

"Wolfe?" Johnny said guardedly. "Sheriff, ain't he? How come he doesn't stop 'em?"

She tossed her head, a bitter smile tilting her lips. Sunlight tangled in her crown of spun-taffy braids. "You *are* a drifter, aren't you, buster? This mountain country is a crazy-quilt. Trying to intercept every isolated raid, or searching these mountains for lost beeves, is worse than useless. Both Mike and the sheriff have taken posses out, but they've lost every trail over rough country."

Johnny glanced at her. "Sounds like some smart

fella's usin' these Hornes' old grudge to break your dad."

She frowned. "But who? Mike didn't build this spread by climbing roughshod over other men—not without a good cause. With the Hornes, he had no choice. They're trash. Their kind squat on a good range and bleed it dry."

Johnny was silent, thinking that it was a hell of a thing for a man of Murphy's caliber to lose the fruits of a lifetime's sweat and blood. Because of his large debt to the Murphys, he had the strange conviction that their troubles were his. Because an owlhoot was trained to look out for number one, he tried inwardly to shrug off this sensation, and failed.

Leonora Murphy came out on the veranda of the big house, and restlessly walked its length to the railing at the east end. She shaded her eyes and peered across the heat-dancing flats, then walked back inside, banging the door.

"Poor Lee," Nan said softly.

"Pardon?"

"My stepmother. She's from a fine Boston family. Mike met her on a trip East a year ago. I guess she was bored with parties, the social whirl, smooth-talking dandies. When she met my father, she was taken with his rough, outright ways. They practically eloped, after her family objected to him on general social principles. But it hasn't worked. This big ranch, with the nearest neighbor ten miles distant, is the opposite of everything she knew."

Johnny said hesitantly, "Your ma?"

"Died when I was fourteen," Nan said shortly.

Johnny, sensing that he'd touched a sore spot, didn't reply. With a sudden insight, he understood Nan Murphy. A grown woman's responsibilities had been forced on her in her early teens. To find her place in a big ranch's lonely men's world, she'd taken on a man's bluff manner. She could talk to a man easily enough, but she'd be lost trying to approach him as a woman. He reckoned that she'd sought his company to talk the loneliness out of her system with someone near her own age. He knew how that could be.

She grinned at him and stretched in a yawn, unconscious of how the arching movement tightened the man's shirt across her small, firm breasts. She straightened her arm and idly rubbed her palm along his cheek. "You don't look so mean without the fur, buster."

Johnny felt hot color rise in his face. He'd shaved off his scraggly beard that morning, and his mirror had showed him a bony, hollow-eyed face beneath a tan turned to sickly saffron. He looked like a curly wolf, sure enough. He thought she was laughing at him now. He said deliberately, "How old're you?"

"Goin on nineteen."

"I'm older'n you. Call me 'buster' again, and I'll pull your pigtails down and tie 'em under your chin."

She flushed angrily; sparks of temper flickered in her eyes. Then, surprisingly, she laughed. "I had that coming."

Then as their eyes continued to hold, something deep and disturbing touched her gaze. The merriment left her face for an expression almost of bewilderment. Johnny understood it no better.

The moment was broken by Mike Murphy's cheery shout. He was riding up from the corrals in a spring wagon, hitched to a pair of splendidly matched copperbottom bays. Johnny knew then that Mike had seen the look that passed between them, for the cheeriness of his seamed, stolid face was replaced by a sudden scowl, his twinkling eyes becoming glacial. Just for an instant. Then his rugged features were composed, his voice normal: "What's the conference?"

Nan laughed. "Mr. Barnes was mad at me, Mike."

"Don't blame him," Murphy growled. "You're a bothersome baggage. Billy, you feel well enough to ride to town? Cook needs a lay-in of grub. I could use an extra pair of totin' hands."

CHAPTER NINE

Jogging along by Mike Murphy's wagon, letting the coolness of the morning work through him, Johnny wondered if it were wise to show his face in Cedar Forks. It was too near Rutherford. Yet he couldn't have objected without arousing Mike's suspicions. So far the rancher had no cause to think that he was other than what he claimed to be, and Johnny meant to give him none.

As they followed the wagon road connecting Tulare and the settlement, Mike talked, his cold cigar bobbing in his mouth, pointing out landmarks and telling their historical tie-ins. Yonder, on his south range, was Murphy's Pass, where Mike had come through the mountains to catch his first glimpse of the basin which he had pioneered. Yonder was the spot where he and Boze had slapped the first Tulare brand on a spavined cow.

"There's the Little Muddy Boze picked you out of," Mike stabbed a horny finger. "All west of the river, far as you can see, is Tulare; east is Miles King's Moon."

"Big spread, Mr. King's."

"Biggest in two hundred miles, except mine.

78

Soon's we cross the river, we'll be riding Moon land almost clear to Cedar Forks."

As they neared the river's flood-swollen onrush, they spooked up bunches of cattle ranging along the river bottom, heavy bellies surfeited with water after weeks of near drought. Among these, Johnny noted, were a few Tulare head; the bulk bore the earmarks and crescent-moon brand of Miles King.

They crossed the crude bridge and drew near the turnoff which led to Moon headquarters. As they neared the road junction, Johnny saw two riders coming briskly along the turn-off from beyond a rolling swell. Mike hauled up the team, bracing them to a stop in the raw mud and giving the horsemen a neutral nod as they cantered up.

"Morning, Murphy." The man who spoke was in his early thirties. His ox-chested frame was clad in black suit trousers stuffed into fine-tooled boots, a white broadcloth shirt with string tie, and an embroidered Mexican *charro* jacket, giving him an affluent, well-fed look. His golden, curling hair was close-cropped under a neatly blocked Stetson. Behind his almost foppish grooming and bored airs lurked a vicious and prideful arrogance which he took little trouble to conceal.

"Howdy, King. New hand, Billy Barnes."

"Looks sort of puny to work cattle, 'less you

use him as a fence rail." This from the other man, a lean-lobo type with a bony clown's face. A small waxed mustache was his one affectation. His well-worn range clothes were stiff and black with grime. He wore a gun in a low-slung, thigh-thonged sheath, which, with his double-rigged saddle, peculiar hatcrease, and drawl, stamped him as a Texan. His shiny black eyes rested with strange amusement on Johnny, and Johnny, with a sickening pound of his heart, knew why.

"Tole Sayrs, likewise new," King said pleasantly. "Murph, you used to be pretty zealous with a smoke-pole, from all I've heard."

Mike shrugged. "You don't build a spread like Tulare without rousting a share of trouble-makers along the way. Unless," he added meaningly, "you have the money to buy the land and cattle to start off in a big way."

"Tole, here, throws a fast equalizer himself," King blandly passed over Mike's comment. "Just for the hell of it, wonder if you could match it?"

Mike shifted his bulk impatiently on the seat. "Sounds like damned foolery to me, King."

"Just a thought. You're packing a side gun. Figure you and Tole could shuck out your shells, no harm done." King paused, then jeered mildly, "Afraid of the past rep?"

Mike glared at him and without a word

shrugged out of his coat, broke the loading gate of his pistol and spilled out the loads. He barely looked up as Tole Sayrs did the same. Johnny felt his shirt cling to his back with a crawl of cold sweat. Keened to such things, he sensed the deliberation behind this. Yet he sat his horse and said nothing as Mike swung down.

Sayrs stepped down, tossed his reins to King, and paced off a distance from Mike. When they faced each other, squared away, King said, "I'll count three. First to pull trigger wins."

Mike wiped his palms on his trousers. "Ready."

"One . . . two . . ."

The bucking roar of a gun drowned King's voice. Dirt erupted between the two poised men. "Billy," Mike bellowed. "What the hell!"

Johnny's gun was leveled on Sayrs, holding the man frozen. "Mr. Murphy, I know this man. He's a gun-tipper. Hires out his iron for pay. You pull against him, you're dead."

"Are ye daft?" Mike sputtered. "You saw us unload!"

"I saw both of you chuck five shells. That figures, man who does a lot of riding keeps his firin' pin on an empty chamber. But I seen this dodge pulled before. Wager you Sayrs's hammer is restin' on a live shell right this minute. Man like him don't draw a gun in play, not ever."

The cold, dead certainty of his words made

Mike hesitate. King spoke dryly. "Didn't know Tulare was hiring wet-eared gunslicks."

Mike shuttled his glare to the man. "I might say the same."

"Rot! I suggested an innocent contest, and this fresh mouthed—"

"Easy to settle," Mike said grimly. "Let's see your gun, Mr. Sayrs."

The man stared at him unblinkingly. He scuffed his feet in the brown earth. "I don't give my gun to no man."

Mike kept walking. His deepening brogue was soft and even. "Ye'll give it me, spalpeen, or I'll break your damned head and take it."

Sayrs's loose-hanging right hand twitched. Johnny's gun crashed again; Sayrs's hat spun from his head. "Let him take it, Tole!" King's wrathful shout came on the heel of the shot.

Sayrs stood in stone-faced immobility as Murphy lifted his gun from leather, broke it, twirled the cylinder. "Aye," he breathed.

"A mistake," Sayrs said thinly.

"Mistake, hell!"

King's voice was silk over steel. "Can you prove it was anything else, Murphy?"

Mike's meaty fist with Sayrs's gun fell to his side. He set his teeth on his storming rage and after a moment spoke in a normal voice. "I reckon I cannot. And it would be too easy to kill either of you with my fists. But this will be remembered. Only *why,* I'm asking. Why, King?"

King's face and voice again held the smooth blandness of utter self-possession. "Didn't Tole say it was an accident? On your horse, Mr. Sayrs."

Jerky-striding, Sayrs retrieved his hat, moved to his horse and swung lankily up. He and King gigged their animals into motion along the road to Cedar Forks. Mike climbed to the seat again, took up the reins with shaking fingers. "With two witnesses, the law would have had to call it an accident. But why in hell would Miles King rig a thing like this? We scrapped some, sure, two adjoining ranches our size are bound to, but—" A sharp lift of Mike's head bore his gaze to Johnny. "You said you knew Sayrs before?"

"I knew him," Johnny Vano said, tight-lipped. "Gun-handy."

"But you, Billy, you just made the handiest draw I ever saw."

Johnny didn't reply.

Mike said now, slowly, "It'd be a small thing for me to ask the why of that, after you saved my life—a smaller thing for me to tell Leo Shallis—the deputy sheriff at Cedar Forks. But I might do it."

"Will you?" Their eyes locked fast, and Mike's were the first to slide away.

"No," he muttered. "In very fact, I'd ask ye

to fork that horse now and ride while the way is open to you, save that I'd do you a worse disfavor askin' you to run than otherwise. Besides," he added roughly, "I now owe you the sanctuary of my roof as long as you want it."

"You hauled me out of the river," Johnny said stiffly. "We're square." He started to rein his horse around.

"Hold on." Mike scowled, chewed his lower lip. "You stay, Billy Barnes. I ask you in friendship, not as an obligation. Whatever you've been, you have the will to do right. I'll take a chance on that, and gladly. Later, we'll see what's to be done. You stay, Billy."

Cedar Forks drowsed in the morning as they cruised down the main street. The only commotion was caused by a brown and white dog who yapped back and forth at the rear wheels as they pulled up at the hitch rack in front of Perrin's General Store. A few loafers lounging on the boardwalk stared incuriously as Mike tramped into the store's spicy coolness.

The long-faced proprietor rounded the counter and shook hands with Mike, then Billy as Mike introduced them. "Howdy, son . . . Say, Mike, I think Leo wants to see you."

"He say what about?"

Johnny's heart thudded sickeningly as Abe

Perrin answered, "Something about that hold-up try up in Rutherford a couple weeks ago."

Mike's thick brows lifted. "News to me. Haven't been off Tulare for near a month."

"Hell, man, whole country's been talking it up. Lenny Wolfe got word that the Vano gang meant to try for the bank. Had an ambush laid for 'em. Nailed two right on the street. Two others got away, one old Sam Vano himself. There was another known member of the gang who didn't show—Jesse Norcross, Sam's nephew. He's dropped out of sight, as has Sam. Lenny threw posses out over the area, got the fella who was with Vano. Shot his horse on the riverbank, but he got away in the water. Blood on his saddle leather. Must have been hard-hit. Drowned, more'n likely. Lenny figured the river'd take his body down as far as your spread. Asked Leo to ask you. Course if you'd found a body, you'd of brought it in." Perrin chuckled. "And you know Leo. Hates to budge from town. Hard to find a horse that'll carry him."

Breath held, Johnny watched Mike inspect the tip of his cigar. Murphy did not even glance at him, only said casually, "Who would this fellow be?"

"Lenny reckoned he was Johnny Vano, Sam's son."

"The devil!" Mike breathed.

"Gospel," Perrin said dryly. "Even the devil

won't want Sam Vano's breed. Sam and his kid rode down a little girl when they made their break out of Rutherford. She lived, but barely. Later, the kid rode back and shot a young bank clerk named Gorman in his hotel room. No one knows why."

Johnny felt coldness ball up in his guts like a chunk of lead. He watched Murphy, seeing him slowly pale beneath his weather-burned ruddiness. Yet his voice held an utter, casual calm: "Guess I better see Leo."

"Yeah. He can supply the details for you."

"Here's the cook's list. See it's filled, will you, Abe?" Only now did Mike look narrowly at Johnny Vano. "Billy, you can start loadin' the wagon."

Mike left the store. Johnny's muscles jerked with the impulse to run, to jump on his horse and ride. Murphy's talk with the deputy would resolve any lingering uncertainty into conviction. Perrin's voice broke into his wild thoughts. "Step back to the storeroom, young fella. You can start with a barrel of flour. . . ."

Johnny wrestled the heavy keg onto the tailgate of the wagon, throwing constant, wary glances at the deputy's office across the street. *You're a sucker,* he told himself cynically. Yet after his first impulse to run, he'd had no doubts about what he'd do. He'd put his trust in Mike Murphy. The rancher had a solid, rooted-in-the-earth strength that commanded trust.

By the time Mike returned he had the wagon bed high-heaped with supplies. The man's face told Johnny nothing. "Should have let me load the heavy stuff," Mike growled, surveying the piled goods. "That everything?"

"That's it."

Johnny didn't breathe easily till they were on the road with the town well behind them. Beyond his clipped query, Mike hadn't said a word. Now he spoke, quietly, flatly:

"I talked to Leo Shallis. Now I want your side of the story, Johnny Vano. All of it."

Johnny talked in terse, dogged phrases as they rode, till the picture filled in for Mike.

The rancher was silent when he'd finished, and Johnny said, shooting him a wary sidelong glance, "You don't figure it happened the way I said?"

"I believe you, Johnny," Mike said kindly. "But the law demands proof. Suppose you could convince a jury that it was Sam, not you, who rode down the child—according to Leo's information, she's crippled for life. You'd still have to prove you killed Emmett Gorman in self-defense."

Johnny stiffened. "Gorman died?"

"Leo said so."

Johnny reined in his horse. "End of the line,

then, and too late to jump freight. Innnocent man hangs as easy as a guilty one."

Mike spoke to the horses, sawed them to a halt. He knuckled his chin in a thoughtful, rubbing gesture. "Yeah. Give yourself up with no witnesses to back you, you'll put your head in a noose sure."

Johnny stared across the brown, rolling land to the serrated rim of misty-purpled mountains. "I wanted to stop. Had a crazy feeling this might be the place. . . ."

"Maybe it can be, Johnny. You said that this Sayrs rode with your gang awhile, that's how he knew you. Any chance he might give you away to the law?"

"Not much, without cutting his own throat. There's a few warrants on his head, too."

"Then only Sayrs and me know who Billy Barnes really is. We'll tell my foreman, too. Between the three of us, I think we can work out this notion that's sticking in my craw."

"You mean—"

A faint smile traced Mike's mouth. He spoke to the horses, putting them in motion again. "What I said a while back, I meant. You could have run out a few minutes ago. You didn't. I got no reason to change my opinion."

CHAPTER TEN

The horse was a sorry, ganted crowbait and the dilapidated hull that Johnny was cinching on matched the animal. But both horse and gear had seen hard usage, and that was in careful keeping with the plan that Johnny, Mike, and Boze had discussed last night into the small hours.

Finished, Johnny swung to the saddle and rode from the maze of corrals across the ranchyard, stopping by the main house where a single saddled horse waited.

Nan Murphy stepped onto the porch, not hiding the vexed concern in her young face. "Boze will be out in a minute," she said, and then, flatly, "I don't like this, Johnny Vano, any of it. I wormed the whole story out of Mike and Boze, and I don't like it."

"Sorry you feel that way," he said thinly.

She stepped off the porch, shaking her head impatiently as she laid a hand on his bridle, looking up at him with clear, grave eyes. "I don't mean it the way you think. I'm glad that you're getting this chance. It's just that it's so dangerous. If there's any other way at all—"

"There isn't."

She bit her lip. "I don't think it's right, sending one man—"

Johnny's voice was unintentionally harsh. "Look, missy, I had to act a grown man by the time I was eight. No choice. I ain't meanin' to brag, but there's few men could handle this game like I can."

"I know," she said. "I'm not saying what I mean to. I—just wanted to say, please be careful. Be very careful, will you?" She reached up a hand to cover his, swiftly, almost shyly, then wheeled and went into the house, half running.

Johnny slowly rubbed his hand where hers had rested and let it fall back to the saddle leather, a flatly denying gesture, thinking, *Don't get ideas.* Several times he'd noticed the hard-drawn tightness of Mike Murphy's ruddy-burned face when he and Nan were talking. The rancher, for all his bigness, didn't want his daughter palavering with an owlhoot, and Johnny did not blame him.

Boze and Mike came out of the house. They shook hands solemnly, without words, and Boze moved over to his waiting horse. Mike moved off the porch and extended his calloused hand to grasp Johnny's. "Good luck, son. We'll be watching for word from you."

The afternoon sun was kind to the buildings of Cedar Forks, mellowing their harsh and warp-walled outlines. It was Saturday. The rigs and saddle horses of farmers and one-loop ranchers lined the tie rails.

Mike Murphy had said that the Horne clan rarely left the mountains, and then only the men, singly, or a few at a time, never in a body. Town held few needs for them: they lived off the land by hunting, fishing, a little hoe-grubbing, butchering Tulare cows. Garth Horne, old man Horne's eldest son, was the only one who came to town regularly.

You could set a watch by the time Garth rode in every Saturday on his herring-gutted roan till snow clogged the high passes. He followed a branded ritual, buying up the family's meager wants—accommodating nearly fifty Hornes for a week—and packing them back to the mountains on his saddle. Before he left, he always dropped into the Alhambra Bar and bought a water glass of whiskey which he nursed along for an hour, listening to the talk but minding his own business.

Boze fished out his watch as they reined in at the main street. "Hold it right here. Don't want to be seen together. If we timed it right, Garth'll be hittin' the Alhambra about now. . . . Sure enough, that's his horse racked in front."

The two dismounted at a tie rail, and Boze's hand tightened over Johnny's arm as he tied up. "Soup's in the fire, son," he said in a low voice.

"Your last chance to back out. Mike's hunch might not pan. And if Leo Shallis should chance to spot you before you leave—"

Johnny shook his head, an impatient negation. "Let's get to it. Give you ten minutes?"

Boze nodded, then angled across the street. Johnny watched him push through the Alhambra's batwing doors. Then, crowded between the horses, he bent his head to hide his face from passersby and pretended to fiddle with his cinch. When he calculated that enough time had passed, he jerked his hatbrim low and crossed to the Alhambra.

He entered a narrow, high-ceilinged room with a bar running down the length of the east wall. The air held a dim coolness that was pleasant in spite of stratified tobacco smoke and an odor of sour whiskey that clung to it. Some farmers were drinking and talking at a rear table. The bar was unoccupied except for Boze bellied against one end and at the other, a tall, thin man of about thirty-five, in buckskins ingrained with dirt and grease drippings.

This was Garth Horne. A tangled black beard hid his face. His eyes were the bleak neutral shade of a fogged sky. There was the untamed look of wild places about him. A tough customer to reckon with, Johnny judged, yet Mike had described Garth as "the soundest apple in a bad bushel," opining that it would be easiest to deal with the Hornes through their least suspicious member.

The fat bartender leaned against the backbar, scanning a soiled, tattered *Rutherford Weekly Journal*. Sweat glistened on his cue-ball head. He looked up with a grunt. Johnny lifted two fingers, then merely stared moodily into his glass after his drink was poured. The pressure beginning to edge his nerves made him wary of drink befuddlement.

He waited for Boze to make the play, and it came soon. He glanced up as Boze moved to his side, simulating a wobbling walk. In a slurred voice: "Kid, have a drink with me."

"Got a drink," Johnny said coldly.

"Have another. Give the kid another, Charley."

Johnny put both hands on the bar and shoved away from it. "Look, mister, he said softly, "just tend your own affairs."

Boze stared at him. "Fresh squirt. Got a mind to take Charley's towel and dry you behind the ears."

"You do that."

Boze didn't reply, just swayed unsteadily. Johnny reached slowly for his glass and sipped it, watching Boze over the rim. "Empty barrel makes the most noise, but it's still empty."

Boze eyed Johnny up and down as if he were making up his mind, then he laughed and lurched away. Out of the tail of his eye, Johnny saw Garth Horne watching, stillfaced. It would establish Johnny's surly enmity toward the Tulare foreman in Garth's mind.

Boze banged his glass on the bar. "Come on, Charley, fill me."

The bartender silently re-filled Boze's glass, and Boze maneuvered along the bar till he reached Garth Horne. He jabbed the man with a sharp elbow. "Hey, Horne, how many Tulare cattle you get last raid?"

Charley said hastily, "Boze, do me a favor—"

Boze gave him a red-eyed glare. "Do me one, Charley. Crawl in one of your bottles and pull the cork in tight. I asked you a question, Horne."

Garth Horne said stonily, "I got no quarrel with you, Hendryx."

"You only think you ain't!" Boze yelled. "Old man Murphy's had me workin' the draws down till dark to find them damn' cows. On your account!" With a jerk of his hand, he sent the contents of his glass into Horne's face. Garth Horne stood stock-still, paling above his dripping beard. Finally he slowly lifted a hand and wiped a sleeve across his face.

"Can't rawhide you to a draw, eh?" Boze bellowed. "Well, I ain't waiting."

He swung from the bar, clawing for his holstered gun. Johnny made an easy draw, the sharp cocking of his .45 freezing Boze's arm before he cleared leather. "Buckskin fella ain't armed, Mr. Loudmouth," Johnny said softly. "Reckon you saw that."

Boze stared at the gun in Johnny's fist, then staggered away from the bar and toppled into a chair, letting his head fall limp on the table. A farmer's chair scraped back in the silence. "I'll get Leo, Charley."

"You stay set, sodbuster," Johnny snapped. "No one's lighting a shuck till I say."

The man stared, his lower jaw falling at something he saw in Johnny's wolf-lean look, then he dropped loosely into his chair. Johnny sheathed his gun and deliberately turned his back on the farmers. He nodded at Horne. "Buy you a drink?"

Uncertainty flickered in the pale eyes. Horne nodded, emptied his glass. Johnny carried his drink over by Horne, waited till Charley had filled Horne's glass, then said mildly, "Happen you might be kin of Jubal Horne?"

"My old man."

"That a fact." Johnny lowered his voice confidentially. "It true you folks'll hide a man for a price?"

Johnny was playing his main hand on Mike's suggestion. Half-savage haters of organized society and its laws, though they'd never openly run afoul of that law till their recent raids on Tulare, the Hornes were rumored to have given sanctuary from time to time to not a few of the

West's most notorious outlaws. From the swift wariness that touched Horne's bearded face, Johnny knew that the hearsay was true.

Horne asked slowly, "Who are you?"

"Name Vano mean anything to you?"

Horne nodded, grunted. "Though gossip, plenty. Hear tell Sam Vano and most of his gang got it when they rode into an ambush up at Rutherford, two—three weeks ago."

"I'm Sam's son," Johnny murmured.

Horne's eyes widened, narrowed to cautious slits. "Yeah? He had only one son, Johnny Vano. I got it the kid was shot and drowned way up the Little Muddy."

Johnny shook his head. "I can show you the hole in my leg. But I made the far shore after I lost my horse, picked up another and some grub at a farmhouse, hid out in the hills."

Horne said narrowly, "Town's a bad place for you then."

"Got tired of lean rations, talkin' to myself. Came in for a drink and to see some faces. Stroke of luck, runnin' across you. Figure you can hide me out till things cool down? Don't want to take a chance, even if the law's got me dead."

Garth Horne scowled darkly, fiddled with his glass between thick fingers.

"Look, I got money." Mike had provided him with a well-stuffed moneybelt.

"Ain't that. Just have to be sure you're who

you say. Otherwise the old man'll buzzard-bait me."

"You want me to go slap the sheriff's face?" Johnny asked angrily. Mike had warned him that he'd have to convince the Hornes of his identity, and Johnny was steeled to meet any test that Garth might demand.

"Just remembered," Garth said then. "We have a fella up there who rode with the Vanos . . . he can vouch for you. I figure you're on the level, just have to satisfy the old man is all."

Johnny shrugged. A lot of men had ridden with Sam Vano, any of whom could identify "Sam's brat." He drained his glass and set it down. "Let's start, then. My back gets crawlier longer I stand here."

CHAPTER ELEVEN

Riding beside Garth Horne, putting the last building of Cedar Forks behind him, Johnny could afford to draw a long, deep breath. The first step was past. The rigged byplay between Boze and himself had duped Garth Horne: from here, Johnny was on his own. . . .

They rode northwest, mounting a vast tableland rolling away to distance-blued mountains.

Johnny had been too busy placing landmarks in his mind to realize how far they'd come; now he saw that the westering sun had crowned the far peaks with rose tinge, the land was beginning to fall into a black outline.

"We come a piece," he told Garth. "Will we make it before sunset?"

"Not quite. But don't worry. I can find our way in the pitch dark."

Shadows of horses and men lengthened into grotesque black specters. The swift twilight had already faded into a soft gray mantle of deepening dusk when they descended the ridge at its opposite end. Now Johnny saw ahead what appeared to be a solid, sheer-faced scarp forming a solid wall against their ingress. Nearing it, he saw that a great, eroded fissure wound tortuously into the rock, and without pause Garth put his horse directly into one of these narrow pockets. They rode single file, shod hoofs clinking ringing echoes along the precipitous walls yawning away to either side.

Suddenly a shout drifted down the canyon from high above. Garth pulled up. A man stood with ready rifle on the lip of the rimrock, skylined as a lone and seemingly faceless figure in the pooling twilight. Garth hailed a reply to the challenge. Satisfied, the sentry pulled back from sight and they rode on.

"Lookout?" Johnny asked.

The dark shape of Garth's head bobbed. "Always one of the menfolk on duty up there. The old man's orders. Takes just one man to hold off an army from that rim. Riders can only come one at a time through this here canyon, in plain view of our man all the way, where they can't get a sight of him. Way the echoes carry, even an Injun couldn't sneak through by night."

Johnny said nothing more, thinking of the impregnability of this mountain refuge. The frowning ramparts tapered gradually lower as they continued, until a sudden turn in the pass debouched upon a rolling, rock-strewn slope falling away from the cliffs to flats of dimly squared fields and meadows: primitively tilled acreage in a wild mountain range. They picked their way down the slope through the growing

99

dark, across a narrow belt of meadow, and into a scattered grove of pine. They rode into a wide, brush-cleared area where a number of small log cabins nestled haphazardly. A door opened; a lank, scarecrow-like man appeared against the firelight.

"Take our hosses, Clem," Garth called. "I got to see Pa."

Johnny swung down, his leg aching with a dull, stiff hurt. He stood flexing it as cabin doors opened and the Horne clan boiled to the doorways to survey the newcomer. Houndtooth-lean men, slatternly moon-faced women, many obviously related by blood to a degree of near degeneracy.

"Come on," Garth told Johnny, and, supplies slung from his shoulder, led the way around a dense hedge of trees that cut off a little nook from the settlement proper. Here was set a lofty log house much larger than the others. Johnny followed Garth inside, blinking at the flickering glare from the stone fireplace. Four men crowded in crude, hand-carved arm-chairs around the shallow oasis of heat and light. Three were lean, dark, younger copies of Garth.

The fourth man was past seventy, but, even slumped loosely in his chair he was well over a great-boned six feet. Age had lean-strung his muscles, stooped and rounded his shoulders. A full, snowy beard hid half his face and spilled like hoary frost over his burly chest. It lent him a benign and patriarchal air that belied the crafty alertness of sharp-blue, still-young eyes. He was shirtless, his gray, cotton underwear grimy. "You git my 'baccy, Garth?" The wheezing voice was like a bucksaw ripping through ironwood.

Garth fumbled in the flour sack. "Here, Papa."

Jubal Horne took the plug, took a clasp knife from his pocket, sheared off a wad, and stowed it in his cheek. Johnny felt himself targeted by the sharp, old eyes. Jubal Horne said nothing, just chucked a thumb at him.

"This here's Sam Vano's son, Johnny," Garth said. With spare phrases, he told of their meeting.

"Easy to prove if he's who he says," old Jubal husked. "Remember that feller you brought here awhile back, Garth? He was a Vano man, proved it with a reward dodger he had of hisself. Bije, you fetch him here. Jump now."

One of the sons stood, stalked wordlessly from the room. Old Jubal gummed his plug with a contented grunt. "Sit down, young Vano. Bije'll be back directly. Meet my other boys, Buck, Eli. You got money?"

Johnny pulled out his shirt and untied Mike's leather money belt cinched around his bare midriff. "Just give it over, son," old Jubal said pleasantly. "I'll keep it safe till you leave. Lot of light-fingered younkers in my family."

Without objection Johnny passed over the belt with all its money, knowing that he'd seen the last of it. It was a small price for acceptance by the clan, and he couldn't afford to antagonize its leader at the offset.

Shortly Bije's gangling figure pushed through the door, followed by a slim man who moved with feline grace. Behind Johnny, a flame-curling log collapsed in the fireplace with an ash-muted *plop*. It sent up high-flaring sparks and threw a diffused, rippling glare across the room, catching on the man's laughing face. Jesse Norcross' voice was a light mockery:

"Fancy meeting you here, Tiger."

Johnny was up at first light of day to inspect the valley. From the pine bench its vast rolling floor fell away in terraced flats, till cut off by the almost perpendicular cliffs that ringed the valley. Even from the bench, Johnny could assure himself that those distant, rugged walls, though bisected laterally with broken shale ledges, would defy the most experienced climber. Yet he felt strongly that there was at least one other exit besides the outer canyon trail. If the Hornes were holding Tulare's stolen stock anywhere, it was plainly not within their home valley.

But for all his hours of keen-eyed exploring, he could not locate the hidden passage in the cliffs which he was now certain existed. Three times he'd watched from his cabin window while Jubal Horne's sons saddled up in the gray twilight and rode from the valley. Always they left by the regular canyon exit, and always they returned from the opposite end of the valley, riding up the terraces around mid-morning.

He was sure only that there was a passage and that it was well camouflaged from even a close observer. He considered waiting by the cliffs some morning to watch for the returning raiders, but there were two solid, rambling miles of the northern ramparts, and one man could not cover all points.

His perseverance paid off on the sixteenth day. He was trekking along a high, shaly bank which flanked the plunging course of a stony stream bed appearing to have its origin somewhere along the boulder-littered base of the escarpment. Johnny hadn't followed it this far before, and now he heard a hollow roar which grew in volume as he advanced. Rounding a place where the stream curved torrentially around the shoulder of a rocky buttress, he saw the white, curving sheet of a narrow waterfall which apparently emerged from a huge crevice at a height of some fifty feet on the sheer wall. It dashed to the rocks below, creaming to wild foam, and here the stream had its source.

With the growing excitement of a sudden realization, Johnny stared at the tumbling cataract.

Scrambling over spray-slippery rocks, he reached a deeply scored niche adjacent to the falls. Standing within the niche, he could see into a gloomy cave. A narrow shelf, just wide enough to accommodate a single horseman or man afoot provided precarious footing between the rock face and the wall of water. He edged along it, till he stood on the white sand floor of the water-hollowed tunnel. Johnny conjectured that two underground streams had once rushed through the wall, working through quake-convulsed cracks, one above the other. The lower one, after ages of pounding out its eroded passage, had gone dry, probably through some change in the upper stream bed. Far down, he could see a distant glimmer of daylight pale the walls.

This was it.

That night, standing by his cabin window, Johnny watched a tight-knit little group riding away toward the canyon exit. He counted five of them. All of Jubal Horne's sons, and Jesse Norcross, too. Another night, another raid.

Only this one would be different, Johnny thought grimly, because he'd be waiting when they returned with their stolen beef. Once he knew where they were holding the cattle, his part would be done. Against the night chill, he shrugged into his ducking jacket and headed for the fenced pasture to get his horse.

CHAPTER TWELVE

Nan Murphy had been cooking and house cleaning most of the day, and she felt begrimed, sweaty and tired. All this trouble for a ranchers' meeting. A day of making the place immaculate for a score of men who would shortly be crowding in, boisterously tramping mud over the carpets and dribbling ashes on freshly swept floors.

Her stepmother had been little help, as usual; Leonora's preparations consisted of spending hours making herself as beautiful as possible. Leonora enjoyed being on exhibit, Nan thought sourly: it was her sole function in life. Nan understood well enough the difference between the world in which she and Lee had been reared to feel sympathy toward the older woman's inability to adjust, but tonight she was tired, irritable, and out of patience.

She stood in front of her mirror, adjusting the white collar of her plain dark dress, thinking of the young outlaw called Johnny Vano as she often had in the days since he'd left Tulare. Long days, during which no word had come out of the hills. He might have changed his mind and decided to throw in with the Hornes: no doubt, their loose, happy-ignorant way of life had its primal attraction.

She remembered how she'd eagerly questioned Boze Hendryx, upon his return from Cedar Forks after seeing Johnny safely in the confidence of Garth Horne. "You should of seen the lad put it over," Boze had said. "Talent wasted. Should of gone on the stage. Me, too." His sharp eyes had questioned her expression. "Plenty worried about him, ain't you?" Yes, Nan thought angrily, of course she was worried . . . sending a man alone among that cutthroat clan. She'd tongue-lashed Mike smartly on that score. "You and your damned maternal eyes," Mike had chuckled. "Hell, Nan, Sam Vano's boy can give those Hornes kings in toughness and draw aces. Don't worry your head about him."

Mother-hen-clucking. Maybe that was it. But hadn't there been something more? She tried to deny it and failed. Johnny Vano's hungry, brooding look had made her feel, for once, like a woman. The moment by the bunkhouse before Mike had interrupted kept returning with its memory of the new, exciting feeling that had swept her.

Leonora entered through the connecting door between their rooms. The older girl wore a white satin gown that left bare the ivory whiteness of throat and shoulders, clinging to the fullness of her upper body and narrow waist before it belled into a full skirt. Beside her, Nan felt thin and angular, and it deepened her resentment.

Leonora said languidly, as she ran a brush through the jet-black shining swirl of her hair, "Would you like one of my gowns, dear?"

Nan eyed Lee's full-blown figure and said dryly, "Thanks just the same."

Abruptly Leonora's lips trembled; the hand with the brush fell to her side. "Can't you try to like me—a little?"

Nan's irritation rose. "Lee, everyone on the ranch has tried to make you feel at home here because we knew it was all different for you. We tried. Don't blame us. What can you do for weakness except pity it?"

Lee bit on her lower lip. "That's cruel."

"It's fact. You had everything. Beauty, wealth, gentle breeding. With all that, a person would expect character. Instead, you flit back and forth like a pretty moth. When you were bored with Boston soirees, you married my father for a pleasant change. But marriage is permanent, Lee. We could forgive your being spoiled and useless; your background made you what you are. But no one admires spinelessness. Mike must have seen something else in you, or thought he did. Enough to marry you. But so far I haven't caught a sign of it."

Leonora dabbed at her eyes. "How can you!"

Nan shook her head resignedly and walked to

the window. From the darkness beyond came the sounds of creaking harness, of men's deep voices. "The men are arriving. You'd better hurry. The moth to the flame, you know."

"Stop it!" Lee's voice carried a sharpness Nan had never heard, and she glanced in surprise at Lee as she arranged her hair into a high, gleaming coiffure, her fingers swift and angry. *I'll be switched,* Nan thought, *I struck fire.*

Maybe that was what Leonora needed . . . antagonism, not sympathy. Everyone had bent over backward to be nice to her. It was possible that a real ordeal might shock her from her pampered shell. . . .

Side by side they walked to the parlor and paused in the archway watching the men throng into the big room. All of them had come directly off round-up; it showed in their run-down boots, dust-caked clothes, and sun-boiled faces.

Mike Murphy stood by the door, the span of his shoulders wedged uncomfortably in his tailored suit. His greetings and handshakes were cordial, until the last man entered. Mike didn't offer his hand; his voice was cool. "Glad you could make it, King."

There was a sardonic twitch to Miles King's half-smile as he gave the women a slight, but courtly-perfect bow. He was dressed fit to kill, his Marseilles waistcoat of white silk and bottle-green frock coat tailored perfectly to his blocky upper body. His boots were of finest morocco leather, polished to a glow. A new pearl-gray Stetson was geometrically angled on his ruggedly handsome head. Nan sensed that King and her father had had a serious falling-out recently, though Mike hadn't spoken of it. But this meeting was important enough for Mike to forego personal feelings: he could not afford to exclude the second largest basin rancher.

"There," Leonora murmured loftily, "is proof that a man can be a real man and a gentleman too."

"King?" Nan laughed softly. "That dress suit with a head on its shoulders?"

Leonora flushed angrily and walked away with a silken rustle of skirts. She began to talk and laugh with King, lightly flirting to show her pique. No one else paid attention, but Nan saw a deep crimson stain lift to her father's face. Mike's stolid Irish Catholic forebears had bequeathed him the firm belief that a man's home and family were sacred beyond even playful tampering, and for a moment she feared he'd explode and throw King out bodily. But after a moment he turned to one of the ranchers and spoke casually, and she relaxed.

Presently Mike turned to the room at large and said loudly, "Sit down, boys."

There was a concerted movement toward

chairs. Some of the men leaned against the walls. An impatient one said, "Let's get to it, Murph. You called this meeting, and it better be important to take us away from round-up."

Mike sat on the arm of a big leather chair, hands on his knees. "Tell the truth, Tom, the notion just come to me. More I thought about it, better I liked it. But with round-up almost over, there's no time to be wasted. Would have been simpler to sound you out individually, but the thing I have in mind is a joint effort." He grinned. "That's a bad word to you boys, but I hope you'll see its reasonableness in this instance."

There were a few appreciative chuckles and a good many stony faces. Nan leaned in the archway, her arms folded, smiling a little as she thought, *He's really grabbing the tiger by the tail.*

Each man in this room owned and ran his own spread. Their ranching statuses ran from wealth to near poverty. Mike himself employed a fifteen man crew; belligerent Tom Davisson, who'd first spoken, worked his own one-loop outfit. If all had one characteristic in common, it was the stubborn independence of backwoods individualists. Mike's statement sounded nearly revolutionary. Nan knew that his real reason for taking this step was his own ignorance of Johnny Vano's fate. He'd expected to hear from Johnny days before, and he could not afford to wait longer and give the Hornes their chance to strike the main blow that would smash Tulare.

"We'll hear you out, Murph," Tom Davisson said gruffly.

"Coming from you, Tom, that is a concession," Mike said dryly; this time most of them laughed. "I'll lay it on the line. . . . We know our herds are being hit by a gang operating from the mountains. Reckon we all know the Hornes are first suspect." There was a general mutter of agreement. "All right. Until such time as we can get evidence and means to stop the Hornes, we'll have to take measures to protect ourselves.

"We work together twice a year as a rule, on fall and spring round-ups. We cut our stock, each man holds his own herd, makes his own drive to Rutherford . . . So far, the Hornes have made small pickings, though these add up. But once our beeves are assembled, they'll likely see a chance to make a bold killing. They could raid a bed grounds, kill the nighthawks, and make off with a whole herd. Something like that might be more than they could handle, but it'd be prime bait, maybe too tempting to pass up."

Nan glanced at Miles King relaxed in his chair as he listened, squinting slightly against the up-furling smoke of his cigar. A faint, enigmatical smile traced his lips.

Nan's deprecating comment about King had been for Leonora's benefit: she did not underestimate the man. In spite of his present prestige, the owner of Moon had come to the territory only five years before and had established himself as a ranching power within two years. His past, the source of his wealth were unknown, though the accepted rumor was that he'd been a Mississippi gambler who'd reaped a small fortune over swift-riffled cards in smoky riverboat salons. It tallied with his slick airs. Maybe, though, her instinctive distrust of King stemmed simply from the fact that she didn't understand men of his dandified cut, of his devious, secretive nature. . . .

"What I propose," Mike was saying, "is that with fall round-up almost over, we pool our herds, riders, wagons and trail gear, and make a concerted drive to market. We'll station armed outriders as flankers, like the military does, and they'll be on shifts around the clock. Every man jack of the crew will be armed to the teeth. No jayhawkers would dare hit an organization like that. Outside Rutherford, we'll split into our own outfits again." He paused. "That's the gist. It leaves a lot of details to smooth out. Just now I want your main reaction."

King lifted his hand a couple of inches. "The idea's all right. Only whose protection will it insure?"

Mike stood, his massive torso blocking out the lighted lamp behind him. "What you implying by that?"

"Nothing, man, nothing." King spread his hands. "I only mean that the rustlers have hit you the hardest by far. For the rest of us, it totals a very minor loss. You'll not take offense at an obvious fact?"

"What about that, Murph?" Davisson demanded.

"I expected that," Mike said grimly. "All right, none of you have been noticeably hurt—yet. But the longer they hit me, the biggest basin rancher, successfully, and get away with it, the bolder they'll become. They'll start to hit oftener and heavier. They may break me. And when they have, d'ye think they'll give up a good thing, once begun? Oh no. Then it'll be your turn. Then it'll be too late to get together and fight back. Alone, each is a sitting duck." His fierce eyes swept them. "Are ye with me?"

"Dammit, yes!" Tom Davisson said. "I like a man who ain't afraid to shoot off his mouth." There was general laughter. One by one the ranchers assented, none eagerly and most of them with reluctance. They began to discuss pros and cons: the joining of herds could be completed in a day . . . the drive begun the next day.

"We'll drink to this," Mike said, "for it's a pact."

"If anyone wants whiskey," Nan put in, "he'll step into the next room. You're not messing up these rugs."

"Hey, Nan," called a young rancher, "how about a walk in the moonlight?"

"Go ahead," she told him tartly, the men roared. They thronged into the dining room, where Nan had earlier prepared a tray of glasses. Mike raised his, toasted the loose partnership, and they drank.

Both women fitted into the man-gathering with rare ease, but in striking contrast. Where Leonora exploited her femininity with flirtatious vivacity, Nan joked and talked with the men as one of them. Behind her easy banter, Nan considered this with irony. Strange how she pitied her stepmother on one score, and was beginning to envy her on another. Stranger still that her own lack of ordinary womanly coquetry had never troubled her before. Not until Johnny Vano had come along. In the face of the realization, she told herself that it was foolish, hopeless, yet she couldn't dislodge the simple fact.

King set his glass down and patted his mouth on his handkerchief. "Strong stuff. I could use a glass of water."

Lee smiled at him archly. "There is water in the kitchen."

She led the way through a side door, King

following. Nan heard their bantering voices, and Lee's trilling laughter. Mike, always too bluff to hide his feelings, wore a fixed glare until they returned, both laughing at something that King had said.

But Nan detected a faint, harried impatience in King's face, and her wonder deepened when King turned abruptly to Mike and said quickly, "Good idea you have, Murph. I'll go along with whatever your fellows decide. Hate to leave so soon, but I got some business hanging fire at the ranch. See you tomorrow at round-up."

He pivoted on his heel before Mike could reply, clamped on his Stetson, murmured to Leonora's startled question, "No, ma'am, I really have to leave. I'll see myself out. Good night, gentlemen, ladies."

The broken-off talk resumed as the front door closed behind King. "What'n blazes is so important at Moon that it can't wait?" Tom Davisson muttered. "That dude rancher always was an odd duck."

CHAPTER THIRTEEN

Johnny blew on his hands and rubbed them. He yawned again. He'd been waiting for two hours. He had easily located the tunnel behind the waterfall with the help of moonglow, and had followed it to its end, coming out in a long-dry wash which he traveled for two miles till it met a high-walled gorge that bit deeply through otherwise inaccessible terrain. On the floor of the gorge Johnny had found much recent cattle sign. He knew that his was the pass through which the Hornes drove their stolen beef, and a moment's thought had persuaded him to wait till the returning raiders came this way, and follow them. In daylight he could have tracked the old cattle sign, but at night the trail could be easily lost in any of a hundred intersecting canyons. By the round-about ascent he'd mounted to this promontory from which he could command a wide view of the gorge.

He chewed some cold jerky from his knapsack, washed it down with a swallow of canteen water, and sat in chilled tiredness while the minutes crawled by.

At last the distant hooraws of riders drifted

faintly downcanyon. Johnny strained his eyes to pick out the specks of cattle and riders against the dark ribbon of gorge. Within minutes they would be out of sight. He caught up his reins, vaulted into leather, and put his horse carefully down the slope.

Shortly, as Johnny had anticipated, the men hazed the cattle up a cross-canyon. He slowed now, picking his way carefully because the narrowly confined walls carried in ringing echoes the clang of horseshoes against rock. This canyon terminated at the brink of a rushing mountain stream. Johnny knew that there must be several such on their backtrail: water left no sign. The riders had driven the bawling animals into the swift, shallow current and were working them downstream.

To spare the risk of being spotted, Johnny left the direct route of the drive and mounted a spur ridge fringed with scrub pine, hoping he could follow unseen along the summit of the ridge. He was in luck, hitting a game trail twisting erratically through the timber.

As the general terrain heightened he left the ridge. His chilled body warmed with the rising sun. Distantly, the faint bawling of massed cattle carried with pine-soughing wind. Feeling a nudge of mounting excitement, he roweled his horse forward and pulled up suddenly almost at the rim of cliffs where it sheered steeply off into a yawning gulf. Shading his eyes against the thin sunlight which washed in a bright shimmer against his eyes, he found himself over-looking a vast park tucked within the mountain heights. Below hundreds of cattle grazed a sun-drenched meadow that unrolled like an emerald carpet to a far periphery of rocky precipices. Almost to the base of the cliffs, flourished a heavy grove of lodgepole pine, and through the feathery yellow-green foliage he made out the gray roof of a cabin.

Then he saw that the Hornes were pushing their horses toward the little cabin. Soon the grove hid them from view, but in a few minutes he saw a wisping of smoke spiral from the chimney. After the night's work they'd rest awhile and have a hot meal before returning to the home valley. Johnny kneaded his reins between his fingers, biting his lip. Get close to that cabin and he might get a slant on their plans.

With Johnny thought was action. He pulled his horse back from the bald summit of the cliffs and ground-haltered him out of sight. He moved through the dense trees, lifting and setting his feet down with silent care. Around the building trees and brush had been cleared away for a dozen feet. He stopped at the edge of the clearing, poising for a short swift run that would take him to the single small, high window on the near wall of the cabin.

Then the door began to scrape open. Johnny settled on his haunches behind screening foliage. Bije Horne stepped out, his whiskers parting in a yawn. He stood for a moment, shoving a hand inside his dust-grimed shirt to scratch his ribs, while his idle gaze circled the clearing. He yawned again, picked up a bucket by the door and headed down a narrow footpath that straggled off through the trees, evidently to fetch water.

Johnny's palms were sweating. He parted the shrubbery, ducked his head, and ran across the clearing to crouch below the window. He pulled off his hat and cautiously lifted his eyes till he could see over the sill, through a dirty pane. Garth, Buck, and Eli were lackadaisically playing cards at the table in the center of the single log-walled room. Jesse Norcross was occupied at the stove.

Garth's lips moved; fragments of speech carried faintly. "Raid . . . King . . . one big drive . . ."

Johnny's skin tingled; his heart thudded dully. Was Miles King's Moon their next major target?

A boot grated behind him.

Johnny started to turn. Bije Horne was there. Sunlight streaked along the barrel of a down-arching six-gun. Johnny threw up an arm, too late. There was a single bursting flare of pain which trailed into numbing darkness. . . .

• • •

Consciousness and feeling returned by aching degrees. He lay on his back in a jumble of harness in one corner, tied hand and foot. Johnny sat up by painful degrees. Over by the table, dark-eyed Bije said, "Shoulda been more careful, Vano. Seen you in the bushes when I come out."

Johnny lay on his back, staring at the sagging roof. A tight sickness gripped his stomach. He'd played a rash and ill-considered game, coming in by the cabin. Now he faced its bitter consequences.

There was a sound of coming horses. The Hornes were on their feet, crowding to the door, their guns out. "Two riders," muttered Garth. "Slack off, boys. It's Papa."

"Will you look who's with him," Buck said. He chuckled.

Horses reined into the yard; men's voices reached Johnny, a creak of leather, the clink of bridle chains. The Hornes moved back from the doorway as their father shouldered through them. His white hair was awry; as his pale-glaring eyes swung to find Johnny, he gave a surprised grunt. He called: "Here's your man, hogtied like a lamb."

Johnny's swift thoughts snagged on an astonished blank. Miles King stood in the threshold, slapping a silver-tipped quirt against his gloved palm. His once-immaculate clothes were dusty and wrinkled; his red-rimmed eyes jumped with a harried impatience. He said slowly, "So you caught him. How?"

Garth told him.

"Good work, boys," King said, his color returning with his bland equanimity. "I rode half the night to tell your father; he had the camp searched, and couldn't find a trace of Vano. We reasoned that either he'd left the valley to see Murphy, or else was tracking you boys here. We rode hard to warn you . . . but this is better than I'd hoped for."

"Don't reckon we follow you," Garth said slowly.

King pointed his doubled quirt at Johnny. "He's a spy for Mike Murphy. He's Sam Vano's son, all right, but getting into your valley was a rigged play to let him circulate freely among you—collecting evidence that could hang us all."

"How d'ye know this, Mr. King?"

King gave Garth a pointed look. "Never mind. The important thing is, he knows. Can't take a chance he'll tell . . . now can we, gentlemen?"

CHAPTER FOURTEEN

Hunched over the table with the Hornes, King sketched his plan. Johnny listened carefully, wondering in the back of his mind what good it would do.

Murphy had persuaded the basin ranchers to throw their round-up herds together and post a rotated guard detail till they reached railhead. King said that wasn't important in itself; he hadn't intended raiding the market herds. The end he had in sight (Johnny wondered what that was) would have come about through slow, calculated decimation of Tulare stock by small periodic raids, and King was satisfied to wait.

But Mike Murphy, without knowing it, had played into King's hands with his notion of tying the herds into one body. Suppose the Hornes could hit the big herd, stampede them back into the hills? The ranchers would recover the majority of course, but meanwhile the Hornes would be rounding up and working small bunches back here. They'd score a *coup* that would shave months off King's projected plans, and more than double the Hornes' present tally of stolen beef.

Old Jubal cleared his throat. "What about them guards, sir?"

King replied that they could toll off the herdsmen by a ruse. Today the ranchers would assemble the big herd; tonight the cattle would be held on a bedgrounds. A number of basin ranch buildings could be fired simultaneously. In this country, bucket brigades were the only counter to a serious blaze, and bucket lines absorbed a lot of men. Fires would be seen from the round-up camp and bedgrounds; men would rush for horses and ride to offer help. The few remaining nighthawks could be easily taken care of.

"Prime opportunity," old Jubal's shaggy head bobbed approvingly. "Take a sizeable crew to hit that hard, though. Need men to set the fires, too. So far just my boys and Norcross have been able to handle the raids."

"You have the say-so with your clan. Draft every able-bodied man. I can join you with my crew of tough nuts."

"Reckon that'll do . . . Tonight, then. And now, sir, I'd planned a rough tally of the head we've already got."

"Good," King said. "We should get an approximation on how badly we've nicked Murphy so far. That meeting he called proved he's coming to the end of the rope—and tonight should turn the trick. Bring your boys and we'll spread out and take a general count. Then I've got to get back to round-up before my fellow ranchers get suspicious." He moved toward the door, his eyes slanting at Johnny. "What about him?"

"He'll keep," said old Jubal, adding ponderously, "This thing has to be, but it's a dirty job, damn if it isn't. Least we can do is give the lad a time alone, to make his peace."

"Don't wait too long, Mr. Horne," King said softly. "Waiting doesn't cleanse a dirty job."

"I said he'll be taken care of," old Jubal growled, "and I'll not renege."

After they'd gone, Johnny lay on his back, trying to think over the battering ache of his skull. *No time to lose your grip. Your last chance; use it.* Setting his teeth against a grip of nausea, he rolled onto his belly, craning his neck upward. On the clay-chinked wall, about waist-high to a standing man, he saw a rusty spoke-long nail sunk halfway into the timber. The tangle of harness on which he sat must have been slung carelessly over it and had fallen off.

With the wall as a support for his back, Johnny maneuvered by painful degrees to his feet. He snagged the tightdrawn turns of rope confining his wrists across the shank of the nail, giving the strands a tearing jerk across the square, sharp-edged head. He lost count of how many times he did this: it was the work of long, aching minutes, tension-strung muscles cramped from his half-bent position and limited orbit of movement. Once he gashed his palm on the nailhead and had to govern his frantic nerves to a harder, steadier pace. Finally he pushed away from the wall, gathered his shoulder muscles, and gave a violent twisting pull that parted the remaining strands.

It was a matter of a minute to free his feet. He stepped to the doorway and halted; a lift of voices told him the men were returning. Johnny lunged through the doorway, across the clearing, running low for the brief shelter of the grove. He heard Jesse Norcross's angry yell. Johnny burst through the dappled glade onto the open meadow and made a beeline for the cliff. A crash of gunfire. Bullets volleyed the tall grasses. He half-turned in his full run. The Hornes, Jesse and King had been making for the shack; now they'd veered their horses to cut him off.

Johnny changed his line of flight to a zigzag run. He reached the ruptured ramp in the cliffs and scrambled to its upper end. From there it was a few seconds to his waiting horse. He hit the saddle in a sprawling leap and kicked the animal into a bolting run. Looking back, he saw the pursuers pouring up from the gully with old Jubal in the lead, his silvery mane streaming, looking like a white-haired centaur.

He heard a shot blast its racketing echo from high away to his left. The two who'd cut off had swarmed over the summit of a ridge and were pushing their horses recklessly down a pine dotted slope, directly athwart his path. Johnny swerved, cut south into the deep ridges. Suddenly he found himself sloping down into the converging walls of a broad cove, which tapered till they dwindled into a deep canyon. With his lead narrowing, he had no choice but to spur into the canyon.

They'd deliberately maneuvered him into this canyon, so it must pinch off somewhere: he was boxed. His rope might get him out of it. Quickly he untied it from his pommel and slipped its coiled length over his shoulder, then slid his rifle from its scabbard.

The men had almost reached the canyon; they opened up with a blistering volley. Johnny's horse shied; he grabbed at the reins and missed as the animal bolted like a released arrow from the canyon. The Hornes' exultant yells rose as his riderless mount pounded past them.

Johnny opened up with his rifle. The men pulled up hurriedly, piled from the saddles and sought shelter. Johnny moved deeper into the canyon at a dogged run. The Hornes followed, but kept their distance, hidden by the twisting walls. He could hear the murmur of their voices, the rash of their boots. They were in no great hurry; they were sure of their quarry.

Suddenly he dug in his heels and hauled up. He knew now: he wasn't boxed, but he might as well have been.

The canyon ended on the lip of a precipice, falling away from his feet for a sheer hundred feet. A hundred feet of smooth, bland sheets and crumbling blocks of rotten shale, eroded by water-burrowed tunnels.

Johnny dropped on his hunkers behind a low, squat out-cropping, watching downcanyon, rifle ready for the final rush. It did not come. They could afford to wait—and to laugh . . . his only way out was straight down. Even with the aid of his fifty-foot lariat, he could negotiate only half of the precarious descent . . . and simple matter for the Hornes to cut the rope before he could get that far.

The minutes passed, and still the Hornes did not close in. They had water and shade. The sun beat heavily on Johnny's exposed back. Flies buzzed in lazy ovals around his head. He licked his cracked lips and clamped an iron control on his panicking nerves. A wrathful determination took its hold on him . . . a man could only die trying.

On his belly he wriggled to the rimrock and looked down. A great rounded buttress of smooth rock whose lower surface curved inward cut off the immediate view below. There was the barest chance that if he could let himself down by rope past that bulge he could find enough broken irregularities to furnish hand-and-foot holds to the bottom . . . and the bulge would cut off fire from above.

He slipped his rope from his shoulder and looped the noose-end over the thick outcrop that had sheltered him. He shook out the coils over the brink, the end dropping out of sight. He let himself over the edge, his body moving down the rope in brief jerks.

He was past the outermost thrust of the bulge then, and was hanging clear of the cliff-face, nothing but a slender line of well-worn hemp between him and nearly a hundred-foot fall to the stone littered base. Less than a yard from his clinging body, nestled in a deep nook beneath the bulge, he saw a broad, projecting shelf of solid rock. He shifted his weight, giving his body the motion of a pendulum. Above, the rush of feet, and Miles King's harshly recriminating voice:

"Damn' fools, he's got away!"

Jesse's excited yell; "He left his rifle. And here's his rope . . . it's jerkin'. He's down there!"

King swore. "Who's got a knife? Here, let me . . ."

Johnny's swinging body was almost touching

the ledge now; he gave a violent thrust of one leg against it, swung far out, and then, arching back, let go the rope and dropped on his hands and knees within the nook.

The rope parted; he saw it fall in a long, graceful loop. With swift presence of mind, he scrambled over to a loose boulder balancing on the shelf-edge. One long straining push sent it over, bounding down the escarpment, setting up a miniature avalanche of broken shale. There was a shattering crash below, and the residual rattlings of falling rock died away.

Buck's hesitant voice carried from above the overhang: "Think we ought to go down there?"

"Why bother?" King asked. "Even if he's alive, he's too broken up to move. Let's go. We've wasted enough . . ."

Retreating footfalls. Voices died away. Johnny sank slowly on his back, letting out his inheld breath.

But there was little time to rest. Get off this cliff. Find his horse. Reach Tulare before nightfall and tell Murphy about the scheduled raid . . . things that had to be done, and any one of them looked near-impossible.

Beneath the ledge, the walls out-tapered slightly at about a ten degree slant. He began to work down, twist his gaze downward to ferret out every crevice or protuberance where he could next put hand or foot. Twice his rope-burned hands slipped from inadequate holds, luckily firm footing saved him. Once a ledge crumbled under his boots and he swung by his arms from a slender pinnacle. He kicked at rotted shale till he secured fresh foothold, then resumed the descent.

When he stood at last on the bottom, his palms were shredded and bleeding. He tore up his ragged neckerchief and knotted it around his hands in a way that would leave his fingers free. Afterward he started a long trek along the cliffs till he found a long-collapsed slide area where he could climb to the rim. Taking his bearings from the sun, he circled north, up and down one high ride after another, forging in a wide circle at a steady, grueling pace till he reached the canyon entrance where his mount had bolted. Hoping against hope that the Hornes hadn't picked the animal up, he began his search.

It was late afternoon when he found his horse grazing in a well grassed pocket. Staggering with weariness, Johnny carefully approached the animal, softly cursing him in a soothing, cajoling tone. He paused long enough to check the girth before dragging himself into the saddle and kicking the animal into motion. Now . . . find the cattle trail. Follow it out of the mountains.

Warn Mike Murphy.

CHAPTER FIFTEEN

It was well after dark when the lighted windows of the Tulare main house came into sight. Johnny approached the ranch layout from the rear, not wanting to be picked up by one of the crew or by a ranch dog. He had to see either Mike or Boze, and both might be on round-up now. But Nan would surely be home . . . He cut through a night-shrouded grove, through a cavernous blackness pocked by scattered patches of dappled moonlight. His horse plodded with lowered head, its breath whistling, on its last legs, he knew. He wondered if his own rubbery limbs would take his weight. Hot food, coffee, a warm bed, swam tiredly through his mind.

He broke from the grove where it bordered a stone-floored patio at the back of the house, illumined by a soft spill of lamplight from windows and the open rear door.

He heard a soft, choked sob. Disbelievingly, he reined in and listened. A woman crying. Then he saw her, huddled alone on a stone bench in the shadows. Her startled face turned toward him. It was Nan Murphy; she lifted a hand to her mouth as if to smother a cry. Johnny realized that she didn't recognize him—small wonder. His drooping horse's once-groomed hide was fouled with dirty lather, his clothes were stiff with dust, his body loose-limbed with exhaustion. A dirty growth of whiskers blurred his lower face below eyes that he knew were red-rimmed and glaring. He must be a hell of a sight.

He swung painfully down, croaking, "Me, Miss Murphy."

The small cry left her then, and he saw her sway forward, then she was close against him, sobbing into his shoulder. Johnny put his arms around her gingerly and awkwardly patted her back, trying to think of something to say. The clean fragrance of her hair filled his nostrils, and all he could think of was that he'd never thought to see this tough-minded girl with her defenses broken.

Suddenly she pulled back, and her voice was steady. "I'm sorry. I guess I was holding too much in. It just broke out—and then—seeing you—"

"Set me back a little," Johnny said lamely. "Never figured you for the cryin' type."

"Neither did I. The trouble in our family . . . I was worried about you. A lot of things."

"Something important Mr. Murphy has to hear."

"Sit down a minute. You're tuckered." Her hand on his arm guided him to the stone bench.

Her breath sucked in swiftly as lamplight fell full on his face. "You've been hurt—and your hands—!"

Johnny felt his pulse quicken with the heightening awareness of this girl. She was wearing a simple calico that shaped her slim body, making her look soft and feminine. He edged uneasily away, not trusting himself. "Tell you about it later."

"What are you afraid of?"

He didn't answer. Her flesh lay warm against his arm. "Johnny," she whispered. He felt his throat thicken as he reached for her, felt her parted lips sigh against his before their mouths met, her pliant strength straining against his body.

They were breathless as they came apart. He said huskily, "No good. Forget it. It just happened."

"You don't believe that. Listen, Johnny Vano. I'm a bossy, aggressive female. I guess—after Mother died, there was something empty in me that Dad couldn't fill. And that's why. I tried to fill it another way, pretending it didn't exist. I never thought I'd feel like this about anyone. If I can, in spite of everything, then it's good, Johnny. It'll last. . . ."

She drew away with a shaky laugh. "I guess I've said enough for now. Mike and Boze came in off round-up for a hot supper. Boze rode on to town to fetch his best gun from the repair shop, but Mike's here. Let's see him."

Mike Murphy was in the parlor, relaxing with an after supper cigar. He greeted Johnny with surprise and pleasure, afterward listening with deeper surprise to his story.

"So King is behind the operation," he mused. "It explains a number of things. If we can get the ranchers organized before those curly wolves come tonight, we'll spike their guns before they know what hit them. As soon as Boze gets back—"

Hoofbeats of a fast-coming rider hit the yard, and a moment later Boze charged breathlessly into the house. Seeing Johnny, he hauled up with a chagrined stare, saying, "Boy, you picked a hell of a time to ride in!"

"What is it, man," Mike snapped.

"Cap'n, I was drinking in the Alhambra when I heard the talk. Some of our crew were in town the other night, and a bartender overheard 'em talking about 'Billy Barnes,' how he came sudden to Tulare and left just as sudden."

"Should of warned 'em to keep it quiet," Mike grated.

"Too late now. They didn't know who Billy Barnes was. But Leo Shallis was in there, and he put two and two together and sent for Sheriff Wolfe. Wolfe got here tonight, and he's organizin' a posse of townsmen. They're like on

135

their way here now. Wolfe'll want to question you. Even if we hide Johnny—"

Mike was already on his feet, reaching for his hat. "We won't be here. Something important's come up, Boze; tell you about it as we ride. Nan, you'll have to stall Wolfe. . . ."

It was after midnight when they reached the round-up camp. Mike Murphy assembled the ranchers and their crews and in hard, flat tones told them who Johnny was and what he'd been doing on their behalf. They accepted the news incredulously, many with outright suspicion.

But because all were basically men of action, they responded with alacrity when Mike called for volunteers. In addition to a reception committee for the Hornes, another group was dispatched in pairs to each valley ranch as a home guard, since there was no way of telling which ranches the rustlers would attempt to fire in order to draw off the herders.

The handiest approach from the Hornes' stronghold was a wide pass through the hilly country north of the bedgrounds. At a point where this pass broadened into a natural bowl, flanked by great slabs of rock and rank chokecherry thickets, Mike dispersed the cowmen. The strategy was simple: stationed in outflanking concealment, they could catch the rustlers in a blistering crossfire. Mike had little hope that it would tide over without gunplay; nevertheless, he warned no one to open fire till the Hornes had been given an opportunity to surrender.

Hours went by, and the cattlemen began to grumble about squatting here half the night on the word of an outlaw brat. Already the night was waning; shreds of gray rifted the eastern sky, the rim of mountains standing out starkly like a ridged black backbone. From the bed-grounds, the distant stirrings of a vast herd carried through the stillness.

A man grumbled nearby, "Wonder where'n hell Miles King and his boys are. Rode out before midnight hell-afire." The ranchers hadn't been told of King's alliance with the Hornes; it would overstrain their credulity.

Boze, positioned to Johnny's left, whispered, "Hist!"

Johnny listened, straining his ears to a sound of muffled hoofs, a creak of saddle leather. Now a spasm of movement in the dimness, a fitful gleam of rifle metal. Next the shadowy forms of riders, emerging like a body of gray ghosts out of a solid bank of darkness.

Mike eased to his feet, sucked a great breath into his lungs, and lifted his cupped hands to form a megaphone. His breath released in a bellow. "You, Hornes! You're surrounded by forty men with rifles! Give up, throw down your guns."

As the last word left Mike's lips, he dropped prone behind his rock. Instantly a shot smashed the silence, ripping air where he'd stood. It was as though the one had set off a fusillade. In the near-dark, it was difficult to place shots with accuracy, but the close-crowded riders made a massed target for ambush guns. Their demoralized return fire was futile; they couldn't break for cover without riding into the teeth of flying lead.

"Every man for himself! Scatter!" Old Jubal's stentorian roar lifted above the roll of gunfire. Johnny picked out his huge upper body straining low over his horse's withers as he wheeled and streaked back down the pass, a handful of others in his wake. He caught Jubal's back in his sights, then deliberately lowered them to the horse's haunches. He pulled trigger, saw the animal's hindquarters collapse. Those behind piled into it and went down in a tangle of harness, kicking horseflesh, and screaming men. Johnny saw at least two riders hurdle the squirming pile and vanish in the fast-graying darkness.

Some of the raiders were already flinging down their guns and throwing arms high in token of surrender. A small group had taken a stand behind a flint outcropping. But it left them inevitably exposed on one side to bullets which poured down like slanting hail.

"All right! Quit! We quit!" Garth Horne stepped away from the outcropping, both hands lifting his rifle above his head. Gunfire died away.

"Let's see all those hands high," Mike Murphy ordered, "and no guns in 'em." With the slow compliance of the raiders who could still raise a hand, the ranchers and their men moved from shelter and came forward to collect their prisoners. Men lay groaning on the ground, unable to stand. Others sprawled silent and grotesque.

Of the Hornes, Buck and old Jubal had not survived the ambush. Eli favored a leg broken in two places by bullets. Garth and Bije stood off to one side, supporting Eli between them, their faces tight-lipped and expressionless. They had made their gamble and had lost.

Boze, rifle snugged in the crook of his arm, fell into step beside Johnny. "Warbag's all laced up, looks like," he said. "No one bad hurt on our side . . . King was with 'em, all right; we got some of his men."

Johnny came to a dead halt. "Not him?"

Boze grimly shook his head. "Few broke out of the trap. He must of been one."

CHAPTER SIXTEEN

King smashed his fist against his knee. How had they known? How *could* they have known? . . . No matter. It was finished. And at the moment, it was little matter to him if he escaped, only to live with a memory of defeat. Until it killed him. And it would kill him, for the inner, overbearing arrogance that was the mainstay of his life was the one thing that all his disillusioned cynicism had never destroyed in him, and now that had received its fatal blow.

With vicious intensity his thoughts veered to Mike Murphy. In a blink concentration of hatred, he fixed all the blame on Murphy. He'd recognized Murphy's voice, calling for a surrender, and it must have been he who'd set up the ambush. King's fingers caressed the cold steel of his pistol. Just one bullet could wipe out the shame in his mind. . . .

He started nervously as a lean figure approached through the mist. It was Tole Sayrs, returning from the summit of a rise where he'd gone to reconnoiter.

Sayrs hauled up before him, his lean, clownish face strangely placid. King felt an envious anger at the way the gunman thrived on danger, and it roughened his clipped query:

"Well?"

"I made out a body of riders movin' east," the Texan drawled. "Reckon that'll be the ranchers, headin' for Cedar Forks with their prisoners. Leaves the way open for us to clear out. But we better hustle. They'll be lookin' for you shortly."

"Not yet, Mr. Sayrs," King said softly, "not yet. First I have to kill a man."

Sayrs' eyebrows cocked quizzically. "Murphy?"

"Murphy . . . a simple matter to cut across country to Tulare headquarters—and wait for him there."

"A damn-fool matter, too," Sayrs grunted. "Allowin' for your feelin's, we'll do best to get while the way's open."

"Do as you please," King snapped. "But I'm also thinking of the Murphy women."

"Come again."

"His wife and daughter, you fool. They'll make prime hostages to see us safely out of the country."

Sayrs grinned toothily. "Sure."

King stood up, "Let's not waste time, then . . . wait!" He palmed up his gun and cocked it. "What's that?"

A shod hoof clinked on stone. A slow-pacing horseman took shape from the swirling mists. He stopped, a few yards away. "King?"

"It's Jesse Norcross," Sayrs said.

Norcross swung to the ground in a lithe movement and moved toward them. His reckless, chalk-white grin was genial, but his eyes held a hint of bridled viciousness that kept King sharply on guard. "So you got away too," King said.

"Figured I'd stick with you, King, You know the country, I don't. You sort of got me into this . . . thought it'd be nice if you saw me out of it."

"You thought wrong, fellow," King said tightly. "I suggest you get on that horse and . . ."

"You do, eh?" Norcross's easy grin hardened as he moved back a step, his thumb caressing light along the worn leather of his gunbelt.

King said through set teeth, "Sayrs."

Norcross's eyes shuttled to the Texan. He said softly, "You sure you can take me, Tole?"

The gunman showed his small, icy smile. "Any time. But hell . . ." He shrugged one shoulder and looked at King. "Three guns're better'n two."

"All right, all right," King said impatiently. "But he'll ride with us under my orders."

"That's understood," Norcross grinned mockingly. . . .

The three of them hunkered in the timber above the Tulare ranch house, watching the front veranda. A body of townsmen sat in the yard, while a big, gray-haired man, one foot resting on the bottom step, talked to Nan Murphy. She wore a gray wrapper and leaned on a fluted porch column, her head shaking in quick negation to something the man had said.

"That's Sheriff Wolfe," King whispered. "Those men must be a posse . . . but what the hell are they doing here?"

At his elbow, Norcross said with an amused malice, "Maybe looking for you?"

King shook his head emphatically. "They couldn't know we'd come here . . . and the bunch that ambushed us were ranchers, not townsmen. They have to be after someone else."

The sheriff's voice, harshened and heavy, bore faintly up the slope: ". . . All right, Nan, I can't wait any longer. But there's something fishy here. When Mike gets back, you tell him to come in and see me, understand?"

He stumped angrily over to his horse, climbed laboriously into the saddle, and rode away with his posse. King noticed only now that one man rode between two guards, his hands lashed to the saddle horn, and he recognized one of his own crew: the man who'd been dispatched to Tulare to fire one or more buildings. Somehow, Murphy had known of that phase of the plan, too, and had no doubt planted men at all valley ranches to foil each would-be arsonist. It was fresh fuel on King's smoldering fury. He said thickly:

"We'll leave the horses here, work in on foot."

With Norcross and Sayrs close on his heels, he stumbled down the slope, keeping a meager screen of timber between them and the house. At a hard run, they crossed the yard that lay open to the veranda. King tramped up to the door and banged on it with his gun-butt.

Nan Murphy opened it, her hand brushing back a straggling wisp of hair. The hand froze, her eyes widened in shock as they rested on the gun thrust almost in her face.

"Move back," King snarled, "before I blow your head off."

Nan pulled aside to let the three men shoulder past. She faced King unflinchingly, saying coldly, "What do you want?"

From the tail of his eye, King caught a movement in the archway at the opposite end of the room. He swung his gun toward it. Leonora stood there, hair spilling in an ebony mass over the shirred collar of her quilted wrapper. Her face was sleep-flushed, her lips sulky and pouting. "What's all the—Mr. King! What are you—"

"Be quiet," King grated. He jerked his gun at the horsehair-stuffed sofa. "Sit, both of you."

Nan obeyed, walking across the room with

her chin high, and Leonora followed automatically, watching King with dazed eyes.

Norcross's light gaze flicked from one to the other, admiringly. "Nice." He chuckled. "No wonder you wanted to come here."

"Just shut up," King said shakingly. His rage dug in deeper at the unsteadiness of his voice. He glared at Nan. "What did Wolfe want?"

"Don't you know?"

He took a step toward her, his gun lifting. "Don't bandy words, my girl. I want a straight answer."

"He was looking for Johnny Vano."

Vano! King's brain rocked with the words. Somehow, Vano must have survived that fall . . . and tipped off Murphy and the ranchers. No wonder they'd been able to intercept every facet of his scheme. "How'd you capture my man?"

"My father sent two men to guard the ranch. They took him."

"I see they did. And those two men?"

Her lips compressed, a twitch of contempt at the corner of her mouth. "You're safe, King. They left with the sheriff's posse."

King considered that. "Just how much," he said slowly, "does Wolfe know?"

"Nothing, except what I told him. That the man tried to fire our house, and that my father would tell him the rest of it when he was ready to." Nan smiled faintly, letting him see the full sum of her contempt. "I'm afraid it didn't satisfy him. He's liable to be back. You'd better make tracks, mister."

"Oh no," King said softly. "We're waiting. Right here. Till your old man comes."

He felt a savage satisfaction at the swift flare of alarm in her face. His words seemed to shock Leonora from her half-daze. She came quickly to her feet, putting out a faltering hand. "Mr. King, you can't—"

Something tension-born snapped inside King. He shifted his gun to his left hand; his right palm whipcracked across her face. "Don't tell me I can't!"

With a low cry, Leonora fell back onto the sofa. She stared up at him, whimpering softly as her fingers touched the thin line of blood from her lip.

Nan said very quietly, "There's your fine gentleman, Lee. A real man, too."

CHAPTER SEVENTEEN

As full, rose-gold daybreak tinted the sky, a loose-strung group of men dropped out of their saddles at the Tulare corrals. The other ranches' crews had stayed at the bedgrounds with the herd while Mike Murphy and his men formed a guard detail to escort the Hornes and the renegade Moon crew to Cedar Forks and Leo Shallis's lockup.

Leo hadn't been there; the old jailer he'd left in charge told them that Leo and Wolfe were on a search for an escaped prisoner. Deciding that this was as good a time as any to turn himself in, Johnny Vano had begun to speak up—but Boze had given him an elbow nudge and a quick shake of his head. Later, as they rode toward Tulare, Boze had said, "You wait. You're beat out. Give yourself a few days' rest at Tulare, then the boss and I'll ride in with you to see Wolfe. He can lock you up if he wants, but he'll sure-hell hear the straight of your story."

At the corrals the crew quickly off-saddled and headed for the bunkhouse to catch a few hours' sleep before returning to the routine of round-up. Mike, Boze, and Johnny tramped up toward the house.

"Presently," Mike was saying, "we'll take some men up to remove the Horne families, the women and children, from that valley. We'll drive our cattle out of the other valley . . . few charges of giant powder'll make certain no one uses them passes that way again."

He glanced at Johnny. "Why so quiet, lad?"

"Trying to figure how to tell you something," Johnny said tonelessly.

A slow frown furrowed Murphy's face. "I think I know. Knew it when Nan and you came into the parlor last night. I know my daughter pretty well."

"All right," Johnny said patiently.

A dry smile flicked the rancher's mouth. "Well, what more is there to say? I know my daughter too well to argue. If it's wrong, she'll have to find out for herself. You too." He paused, rather uneasily. "Just meant to say, you're both pretty young. Do an old man a favor, wait a while. Be sure. Do that?"

Johnny answered him bluntly. "All right, Mr. Murphy, but it won't change anything."

Mike glanced at Boze's long, grinning face, then said humbly, "No, guess it won't. And I guess, at that, I ain't sorry." He hesitated. "You be good to her. She's all—" He broke off then, saying gently, "I reckon you know, son."

They reached the veranda and tramped onto it, self-consciously stamping dirt from their boots against womanly injunctions. Johnny's pulse quickened at the knowledge that in another moment he would see Nan. . . .

Mike reached for the doorknob; it turned before his hand closed on it: the door yanked open. A gun gleamed in the hand of the man who stood there. His urbane tones grated with an inheld tension. "Come in, by all means do, gentlemen."

Like stunned automatons, the three men shuffled across the threshold, past Miles King who stepped back to let them enter, his gun on-cock and ready. Though it was full daylight now, a lamp burned unnoticed on a small table. Johnny felt a tug at his hip and half-turned to meet Jesse Norcross's flashing grin. Jesse rammed the six-shooter he'd lifted from Johnny's holster into his own belt, giving Johnny his old, cocky salute. "Howdy, tiger."

Jesse here!—with King . . . Numbly, Johnny stumbled against the wall, propelled there by Jesse's rough-prodding gun in the small of his back. There was Tole Sayrs, too, lounging against the fireplace, one arm hooked over the mantelpiece, the other hanging loosely at his side. A cold twirly dangled from his lips; his ice-calm face showed nothing at all. He hadn't troubled to pulling his gun, and Johnny, remembering Tole's ability with a sidearm, understood his composure. Even with his Colts in leather, Sayrs was the one to watch if gunplay started.

King took Mike's gun, and Boze's, and pushed them over beside Johnny. Johnny turned to face the entire room now, seeing Nan and Leonora huddled together on the divan. Nan seemed composed, her only mark of tension a restless movement of hands; she managed a smile for him. Likely she'd been comforting the older woman. The color was drained from Leonora's tear-streaked face. Johnny wondered narrowly if either girl had been manhandled: Leonora's lips looked cut and swollen.

Mike's blue-bright gaze ranged from his wife to King. He began thickly, "Damned divil, if you—"

"You'll do nothing," King said wickedly, his pistol centered on Mike's chest. "You're holding aces and eights right now. I'd hate to end it so soon—but I can. Any time."

Mike's weight, forward poised on the balls of his feet, settled back onto his heels, his breathing gusty and hard drawn.

"That's better. I'd hate to finish it now when I can watch you sweat a while. Time doesn't matter much, now. It did, of course. The sooner you were dead, the better. Later, as Tulare went under from continued rustling losses, your daughter and widow would be eager to sell out, cheap."

Boze cleared his throat gently, his voice surprisingly mild: "This Sayrs fella was to finish Mike?" Johnny glanced quickly at Boze, caught the foreman's eye fleetingly: Boze was stalling for time, and now Johnny sensed his unspoken message: You're younger and faster than me, son. Think of something, but think fast. When you make your play, make it good.

King grimaced, "I hired Tole for that purpose . . . a killing which would seem like an accident. The first chance we got. But when it came, Vano, there, saw through it." Moving on to Johnny, his eyes looked cruel, yellow-sheened by the lamplight. "Vano is too smart for his own good."

Boze persisted, "All along, you were really after Tulare?"

King laughed with an unsteady timbre and began pacing the room back and forth. ". . . Sure, but not solely for the ranch itself. Hell, I'm a gambler, not a cattleman. And no gambler ever played for higher stakes. The Hornes' mountain set-up tied in perfectly; with their help I could have kept hitting the lowland ranches indefinitely. My own problem was where to ship the cattle. Rutherford couldn't be risked, even with clever job of venting the stuff to my Moon brand and forging bills of sale, and I'd have to drive across this basin to get there.

"Railports to north and east are hundreds

of miles away, across the ruggedest mountain terrain in the territory . . . out of the question. But Murphy's Pass, on Tulare's south range, cuts deep and wide through the bad country and would give me access to far southern railroad towns, where I could market without suspicion because the basin ranchers always drive to Rutherford, a lot nearer. From that strategic point I could bleed the basin dry."

Boze nodded calmly. "Ahuh. You had to have Tulare first . . . that's why the Hornes were hitting us nearly exclusive. Spliced in neat with their old grudge against Mike. You used them, they used you."

King shrugged indifferently, looking restlessly away. Johnny sent a swift sidelong look at the still-burning lamp on its table: that might be the answer, if he could edge nearer.

"Still don't know how you learned about Johnny," Boze added.

King laughed. "Why, Murphy's little idiot of a wife. Who else?"

Mike's face darkened with a lift of tidal blood. He took a step toward King, saying softly, "You blackleg liar."

"No, Mike," Leonora cried. "It's true."

"What!"

"I didn't mean . . . I didn't know. The other night, when King and I stepped into the kitchen, he asked about the reason for your calling an abrupt meeting. I knew you'd cautioned me not to breathe a word about Johnny Vano spying out the Hornes, but I was mad at Nan and I—I wasn't thinking. And I couldn't see the harm in telling King. He—he—"

"Yes," Nan interrupted, "he seemed like such a gentleman. I'd badgered Lee about that . . . and I guess I'm as much to blame."

"Touching," sneered King, "this familial loyalty . . . very."

Johnny shifted his feet with seeming restlessness, a side-stepping movement carrying him a foot nearer the lamp. Jesse lounged over and rammed his gun muzzle into Johnny's short ribs. "You act sort of skittish, tiger. Best stand easy. Wouldn't want you to keel over of heart failure before I do the job."

"You want to kill me, Jess?"

Bantering mockery fled Jesse's face, exchanged for a cold, killing hatred. "Still in the dark, are you? Still think it was Gorman who tipped off that bank job?"

Johnny's flesh chilled as though a wintry draft had swept the room. "*You?* You, Jess?"

"Me." Jesse's face pinched with a long-stored malignancy. "Sam Vano was rough on you, but he was groomin' you for the leadership. Heard him tell Bowie so, once. And Bowie was your friend. For me, nobody ever gave a damn, not ever. You know what my ma and pa was. The gang had got to be a habit, that's why I hadn't broke away before. Only that night before the job, when Sam hit me, that tied it. I was through, and I was goin' to make him and the damn' lot of you pay. When you and me was in Gorman's room, I planted the hunch in your head that he might cross us for the head money— so in case the ambush failed, the gang would put the blame on him. Later, when you were asleep, I sneaked out of the hotel and left a note under Wolfe's office door. Oh, make no mistake, Tiger . . . I'll enjoy killin' you."

"Don't talk, Norcross, do it," King put in harshly. He steadied his gun on Mike. "Tole, you take Hendryx."

Boze said in a tight, quick way, "Shots'll bring the whole crew up here on the run. You overplayed it, King."

"On the contrary. Our hostages will see us safely past your men."

"Hostages?"

"Why yes," King grinned tightly. "Our hostages will be our hostesses. What do you think of—"

"Why you damned—" It left Boze on an explosive breath. His lean body launched in a low-driving tackle at King. The man flinched back involuntarily, then pulled trigger. The gunshot, confined by four walls, crashed deafeningly. In mid-lunge, Boze was hammered back in a twisting fall.

Instantly, Johnny moved. With a cuffing swing of his arm he sent the lamp flying from the table, crashing in the center of the room. A reeking flood of kerosene sprayed over the carpet; a tiny flame caught, sent a broad sheet of flame ripping across the floor with a wildly diffused flare of brilliance.

Already Johnny was flinging himself sideways into the startled Jesse, hitting him solidly, grappling him around the waist, gun hand pinned to his hip. The impetus carried them both into the little table, and it gave under their weight and crashed to the floor with them, Johnny on top. Pinning Jesse's elbows with his knees, he yanked his own gun from Jesse's belt and clubbed the fisted weapon to his jaw. Jesse's muscles strung hard in brief protest, then went limp.

Johnny scrambled to his feet, pivoting to face the room. He saw that Mike Murphy must have moved almost as fast as himself, for he'd caught Miles King around the chest in a crushing bearhug, the hand with the gun twisted up behind him at an agonizing angle, contorting King's face with wrenching pain. The two men swayed back and forth between Johnny and Tole Sayrs— the only thing, Johnny knew, which had kept Sayrs from gunning him as he was occupied with Jesse. That, and the high-leaping swath of flames which blocked Sayrs off, his back to the fireplace.

Then a violent heave of King's body carried him and Mike burgeoning away, crashing into the wall with an impact that shook the room. It cleared the space between Sayrs and Johnny. The Texan's hand blurred down, slapped pistol grips and whipped to level. Automatically, smoothly, Johnny swung his gun up, thumbed the hammer and fired, aiming with his eyes. The recoil smacked the butt against his palm. Sayrs grunted in pained surprise, and started to reel forward. He got off a shot which slammed wide of its mark. Then he dropped his gun and toppled forward, straight-stiff as a felled pine, across the blazing carpet.

Johnny's gaze flicked on to Murphy and King. Two big men wrestling for a gun which sawed dangerously back and forth between them. Their struggles carried them in tussling, turning confusion across the room and back, making it impossible for Johnny to help Mike. Suddenly the gun exploded. Mike stumbled away, and Johnny saw that he held the gun. King was bending over, his fists doubled against his belly, an expression of utter disbelief filling his face, pulling his mouth into a lolling slackness. Then the face went blank and he dropped to his knees, pitched full length on his face.

Johnny caught a glimpse of Nan on her feet, her fists clenched at her sides, and he shouted hoarsely for her to stand aside as he reached a far wall, ripped up an edge of carpet and with a desperate heave of strength that carried the furniture before it, flung the end he held over the burning part, folding back on itself to smother the flame. Clouds of smoke mushroomed out, lifting pungently, blindingly, through the room. Coughing, tears streaming from his eyes, Johnny stumbled to the door and threw it open.

As he turned back inside he stopped cold.

Jesse had been playing possum. Watching his chance, he'd lunged to his feet and caught Nan, his arm bent in a choking hug around her throat, the muzzle of his gun pressed to her temple. Sweat beaded glisteningly on his face as he backed toward the archway leading to the dining room. Mike and Johnny stood rooted, helpless.

Johnny said huskily, "Give it up, Jess. You're done."

"Not yet, tiger . . . one more hand to fill."

He attained the archway, and for a moment lowered his gun to Johnny. "At least I can take you—" Nan gave a hard twist of her slim, wiry body; it carried them off balance. To keep his footing, Jesse had to let go, flinging her aside with a sweep of his arm. Then he snapped a wide shot at Johnny, spinning on his heel as he fired and bounding like a cat through the archway. Johnny heard his pounding footfalls echo through the house, the back door slam.

There was a confused outbreak of yells and scattered shots across the yard. He saw the crew, some of them half-dressed, taking cover behind the corrals as they blazed away at the half-open doors of the stable.

Luke Mayerling turned his gaunt head as Johnny came up. "Heard shots," the old puncher said. "The lot of us came pilin' out of the bunkroom, saw this fella makin' for the timber. We cut him off, he run into the stables. Cornered there . . . Say now, that shooting—"

"Everyone's all right," Johnny broke in to save talk. "Tell the boys to hold fire, Luke, I'll take him."

A sound of running feet brought Johnny around to face Nan Murphy. Breathlessly, she caught his arms. "Johnny, you've done enough. Don't—"

He shook his head like a ringy bull. "You hear me, Luke? Tell them to hold fire. This one belongs to me."

CHAPTER EIGHTEEN

The wild, ugly passion that boiled in him must have shown in his face because Nan pulled away from him, and stepped back. "Is this the way you'd planned to change, Johnny Vano?" she asked almost inaudibly. "You're not thinking now of bringing a criminal to justice. Only of shooting a man in revenge."

"Quit it," he said thickly, doggedly.

"Johnny, Johnny, don't you understand, even now? Making yourself over isn't only doing, it's feeling. If you kill a man for your reason, you'll be no better than a murderer!"

"The order, Luke."

Luke bawled a command, and the peppering of gunfire died. Johnny expected Nan to protest again, but now she held an almost condemning silence as he moved away, gun drawn, into the labyrinthian cross-hatching of corral poles which would give him partial shelter till he was close to the stable. He ducked low and started running down a narrow runway. It brought him to a cornerpost where the corrals ended. Across a narrow space beyond lay the stable, its door barely ajar.

He crouched by the post, watching the murky patch of shadow between door and jamb, till his vision was spotty and aching. The sun slanted hot against his back. Was Jesse waiting just within the doorway, to put a bullet into whoever came after him? Breath held, he took a cautious step that exposed his shoulder and part of his arm. A purple-orange tongue of flame licked from the doorway. The bite of the bullet gnawed wood-shards from the post.

Johnny opened up, blasting at the muzzle-flash. He heard a rush of feet in the stable: he'd nicked or scared Jesse into retreating deeper into the building. Johnny lunged into the open, reached the door, kicked it wide with a sweep of his leg, and dived through, hitting the floor on his shoulder and rolling across the gangway, into a stall between two partitions. A pistol spoke from the shadows at the other end of the building. Johnny heard the slug boom into the planking: a high miss, and he knew that Jesse was shooting blind.

He sprawled on his belly, his face barely exposed around the edge of the partition. The cedar stock-plates of his gun lay warm and moist against his palm. A stir of wind banged the door shut, throwing the interior into almost complete gloom. Johnny's body jerked, nerve-strung with the sound, and slowly relaxed, constrained to waiting. Jesse and he were on level terms, each alone in the darkness, but Jesse was the cornered one; Jesse would break first, make the movement or sound that would give his enemy a target.

Though the stable was empty of animals, the rank smell of manure filled his nose suffocatingly. A familiar smell, but heavy and nauseating, here on the dank stable floor. *Watch,* he thought. *Watch, and don't think about it.*

About what, then? What Nan had said? All right, he had to face it. But how, how could a man shed the harsh lessons, the warped, deep-rutted feeling-values of a lifetime in a few short weeks? Always in his past, there had been only the code of the gang, the law of any wolf-pack. An eye for an eye. But a man has a choice, Sam Vano, dying, had said. Johnny had ignored it then, and a thirst for vengeance had led to the killing of Emmett Gorman. Nan had said it another way: *Making yourself over isn't only doing, it's feeling.*

Restlessness needled him; he steadied with an iron effort. Jesse had more patience than he'd credited him for. How many loads remained in Norcross's gun? He hadn't had time to reload, and he couldn't do so now without making a giveaway noise. He'd fired three times at Johnny. Three expended shells that Johnny knew of, perhaps more. Assume an empty sixth chamber.

Give him a maximum of two shots, then. Make him use those and you've got him. With infinite care, Johnny pulled himself into a crouch, unfastened one of his spurs. An underhand toss sailed it down the gangway. It made a clear, metallic *chink*. Jesse's nerves must have been strained to breaking; he blasted away wildly, firing twice before the futile click of hammer on an empty chamber.

Johnny stood, but didn't stir from his small niche. "Five shots, Jesse. Throw your gun out, you follow. Or I come after you shooting."

Dead, oppressive silence to which Johnny listened uneasily. It was a reaction unlike Jesse. He might have cursed, wept . . . anything but this.

Then, softly, but with a note of harried desperation: "Here it comes, tiger." The gun skidded down the clay floor of the gangway and stopped in a bar of sunlight from a crack in the warped siding. Johnny gave it a spare glance and said grimly, "Come ahead now, Jess."

He caught the tracery of a shadow inching forward, and waited till a faint glint touched gun-metal at midheight on the shadow, snugged in half-concealment against its hip. Johnny tilted his gun a bare degree to the left, and sent his shot thundering off. The shadow screamed; the gun it held spewed flame into the floor. Then the shadow was gone, and it took a few seconds for Johnny to see that it had dissolved onto the floor.

Guided by the downed man's groans, Johnny moved to his side, gun held ready while he located a match with his left hand, snapped it alight on his thumbnail. The saffron flare showed Jesse on his back, eyes glazed with pain, his hand twisted in his bloody shirtfront: Johnny knew without looking that his shot had only scraped the ribs. A double-barrel pocket pistol, small enough to be concealed in boot or shirtsleeve, lay by Jesse's arm. Johnny murmured, "Crooked hand straight to the last deal, eh, Jess?" as he kicked the little pistol across the gangway, sheathed his gun, and blew out the match.

He bent over, slung Norcross's arm over his shoulder and steadied him to his feet, supporting the groaning, feebly struggling man to the door, which he nudged open with his foot. As they emerged into the glaring sunlight, the crew surged forward, and with them, Johnny saw, lumbered the rolling bear-shape of Sheriff Wolfe. But Nan, running as lightly as a young boy, was the first to reach him.

He pushed Norcross into the arms of the crew and turned to her. "It's over, Nan," he said wearily, "it's over, and I didn't kill him." She leaned against him with a sob of relief.

Wolfe came up, pale eyes snapping below

his bristling scowl. Leo Shallis was at his side, with Mike Murphy following, his broad face deeply calm. The sheriff grabbed Norcross's wrists and clamped on handcuffs, and then, glaring at Johnny, snapped his fingers at his deputy. "Loan me your cuffs, Leo."

"You won't need 'em," Mike said softly. "Not for Johnny."

The sheriff drew a long, sighing breath, as though fighting for self-restraint. His face looked nearly apoplectic. "What the hell," he got out, "*is* this? You been protecting Vano—unless Boze gave him a hand last night on his own account, and I doubt that. When I questioned Nan, a while ago, she was too damned evasive to suit me. That's why I came back. So kindly tell me just what the hell's going on."

Mike smiled wearily. "Come on to the house. I won't tell you, I'll show you. . . ."

An hour later, Leonard Wolfe was striding up and down the front room, a touch of buoyant elation in his step, his craggy face more than mollified: he'd heard out Mike and Johnny and even Boze, who, conscious now on the sofa, had insisted on adding his bit in a shaky but strong voice. Sam Vano's death was confirmed, the last of his gang rounded up. The Hornes were jailed, awaiting trial. In a wagon outside lay the tarp covered bodies of King and Sayrs, and Jesse Norcross, his torso swathed in bandages, sat beside them handcuffed to the tailgate.

Mike, sitting at his ease by the fireplace, was saying, "Johnny understands he's got to stand trial for shooting that bank clerk up in Rutherford, Lenny. But there was an exonerating fact or two I think you should know. . . ."

Wolfe, hands clasped at his back, swung his gaze onto Johnny and Nan, standing self-consciously by the door. "Yeah. I know. Gorman lived a while. Confessed everything to accredited witnesses before he died. Among other things, that you shot him in defense."

Even in the overwhelming sense of relief he felt, Johnny could not ignore another nagging guilt with which he'd lived these many weeks. Hesitantly, he said, "The little kid Sam rode down . . . it true she'll never walk again?"

"Afraid so, son. Operation by a specialist would turn the trick, but her folks ain't got that kind of money."

Johnny let out a shuddering breath. "I'd given ten years of my life if I could set that right."

"Let's say, all your life," Mike murmured, somberly, but his tight-set lips struggled with a smile. "You'll serve out the sentence right here." At Johnny's bewildered look, Mike grinned, "I'll pay for the operation . . . a sort of jump-the-gun wedding present."

Wolfe reached for his hat on the mantel-piece, saying, "Better get our prisoner to town. Come on, Leo." Shallis grunted to his feet and waddled after him.

Johnny stepped squarely in front of the sheriff as he started past, saying flatly, "You'll be wanting me."

"No hurry, son. Come in when you're ready." He winked soberly. "If anyone asks, I didn't know you."

Mike called after them, "Send Doc Stone out to look at Boze."

"I'll send him back with your wagon." Wolfe followed Shallis onto the high, creaking wagon seat; Shallis took up the reins and shouted the team into motion.

Mike came to his feet and walked to Leonora who was wiping Boze's perspiring face with a damp cloth. She'd been in a state of half-shock for some minutes after the violence had ended, then had roused herself silently and without a word had helped Nan dress Boze's shoulder wound.

"Lee," he said awkwardly.

She looked away from him. "Don't say it, Mike." Her words were low, toneless with a husky remorse. "Mr. Vano was almost killed because I acted like a sulky schoolgirl. Anything you could say wouldn't say the half of it."

"Lee," Mike said gently, turning her to face

him. "You're my wife. We have a duty to understand each other, not condemn. Reckon we can start with that."

"Mike." Her eyes radiant through tears, the old, sulky discontent gone, made Leonora really beautiful, then.

This Johnny Vano noticed in passing. He drew Nan out onto the porch, then, aware of his ragged, filthy condition, let his hand fall self-consciously. Through a haze of exhaustion he considered all that he wanted to tell her, and could not think how to begin.

"So much has happened," she said in a hushed voice. "I wonder if we can forget it."

"Maybe," he said, searching for his words, "we'll be the better for remembering, all of us." He looked at her obliquely. "Your dad wants us to wait. Be sure, he says."

A mocking little smile touched her mouth. "You're not sure, Johnny?"

"Sure I'm sure. I just—"

"Why, then, that's all we need," Nan murmured, and came into his arms.

Center Point Large Print
600 Brooks Road / PO Box 1
Thorndike, ME 04986-0001 USA

(207) 568-3717

US & Canada:
1 800 929-9108
www.centerpointlargeprint.com